RUNNING
through
SPRINKLERS

RUNNING
through
SPRINKLERS

Michelle Kim

ATHENEUM BOOKS FOR YOUNG READERS
New York London Toronto Sydney New Delhi

ATHENEUM BOOKS FOR YOUNG READERS

An imprint of Simon & Schuster Children's Publishing Division

1230 Avenue of the Americas, New York, New York 10020

This book is a work of fiction. Any references to historical events, real people, or real places are used fictitiously. Other names, characters, places, and events are products of the author's imagination, and any resemblance to actual events or places or persons, living or dead, is entirely coincidental.

Text copyright © 2018 by Michelle Kim Mossop

Illustrations copyright © 2018 by Alexandra Huard

All rights reserved, including the right of reproduction in whole or in part in any form.

ATHENEUM BOOKS FOR YOUNG READERS is a registered trademark of Simon & Schuster, Inc.

Atheneum logo is a trademark of Simon & Schuster, Inc.

For information about special discounts for bulk purchases, please contact Simon & Schuster Special Sales at 1-866-506-1949 or business@simonandschuster.com.

The Simon & Schuster Speakers Bureau can bring authors to your live event. For more information or to book an event, contact the Simon & Schuster Speakers Bureau at 1-866-248-3049 or visit our website at www.simonspeakers.com.

Also available in an Atheneum Books for Young Readers hardcover edition

Book design by Debra Sfetsios-Conover

The text for this book was set in Adobe Jenson Pro.

Manufactured in the United States of America

0719 OFF

First Atheneum Books for Young Readers paperback edition April 2019

10 9 8 7 6 5 4 3

The Library of Congress has cataloged the hardcover edition as follows:

Names: Kim, Michelle (Filmmaker), author.

Title: Running through sprinklers / Michelle Kim.

Description: First edition. | New York : Atheneum Books for Young Readers, [2018].

Identifiers: LCCN 2017005310

ISBN 9781481495288 (hardback)

ISBN 9781481495295 (pbk)

ISBN 9781481495301 (eBook)

Subjects: | CYAC: Best friends—Fiction. | Friendship—Fiction. | Self-actualization (Psychology)—Fiction. | Racially mixed people—Fiction. | Family life—Canada—Fiction. | Canada—Fiction. | BISAC: JUVENILE FICTION / Girls & Women. | JUVENILE FICTION / Social Issues / Friendship. | JUVENILE FICTION / Social Issues / Adolescence.

Classification: LCC PZ7.1.K583 Run 2018 | DDC [Fic]—dc23

LC record available at https://lccn.loc.gov/2017005310

For my family

and

for all my girlfriends, past and present.
Especially you, Dany Lee. Magic World Forever.

RED MAPLE TREES LINE OUR CUL-DE-SAC
like candles on a birthday cake. Close your eyes and
make a wish. You could probably blow all the candles
out. The trees here aren't as big as the ones you'd find
in Vancouver. Here, in the suburbs, in Surrey, the trees
are younger—weaker, even. So small and thin, they
need wooden stakes strapped to them to keep them from
slouching over. So small and thin, they flicker when the
mail carrier walks by.

A letter slips through the mail slot. It is from my best
friend from across the street. You see, we figured out this
scam. Actually, she figured it out. It's a good one, so listen
up. She got this idea of trying to send me a letter without having to pay for a stamp. So instead of writing her
address as the return address, she wrote mine, instead.
The post office people probably got angry, thinking, You
idiot, you forgot the stamp, here's your stupid letter
back. Only thing is, the letter ended up at my house
instead of hers. And that's just what she wanted.

All the letter says is:

Dear Sara,
Muahahahahahahaha!

Isn't she the best? She always has been, for as long as I've known her, which has pretty much been my whole life. So when I learned the big news, it gave me this real bad feeling inside. *Nothing is going to change,* she promised me.

But that was the year everything changed. It was the year I lost my best friend and witnessed the biggest missing persons case in Canadian history unfolding right in front of me. It was also the year I almost lost myself.

When they first built suburbs outside Vancouver, it's as though they thought that the sameness of everything would keep the outside world away and the rest of us safe inside. But the thing is, change happens from the inside out, too. So when last summer came to an end, just before my final year of elementary school, my twelfth year in this world, not even the perfect roundness of the cul-de-sac could help me.

1

IT'S AUGUST and the refrigerator is Nadine Ando's dance partner. She puts her hand through its handle and swings it open to cool her body down. Plants her right foot on the floor, pulling her left leg behind her, her toes a perfect point. Then in one swift motion, she flips over and bends into a backbend and shows off her belly button to the ceiling. A dip into the clear bin, VEGETABLES, and then she comes up with one single carrot.

"I'm on a diet," she says, and walks over to the kitchen table, where I am.

Me: "Why?"

"Just trying to be healthy," she says. *Crunch. Crunch.* "What are you eating?" *Crunch.*

I look down: Steaming-hot ramen noodles with ice cubes swimming in a salty, beige soup. The ice cubes are a trick I use to cool the soup down just a bit. They make large oily swirls around the white noodles. I like how the noodles look, blond and crimped, like my old Cabbage Patch Kid's hair.

Jen, in the hall: "Hey, didn't you eat, like, half a chocolate cake last night?" Jen is Nadine's sister. She's ten, a year younger than us. "Diet, my butt!" she says.

Mrs. Ando, somewhere in the house: "Everyone in the minivan now! And, Jen, watch your language! Christ."

In the grocery store:

Mrs. Ando, Nadine, Jen, their little sister Megan, and me. Mrs. Ando is pushing a shopping cart down the canned-soup aisle. She picks up a can of clam chowder. Nadine gives me a look, as if saying, *I hope that's not tonight's dinner.*

She cups my elbow and whispers, "Let's go."

We run. Race ahead to the meat section, guessing which part of the cow's body is mushed-up behind the plastic wrap. To the vegetable and fruit section, little sprinklers spraying a light mist on our faces. To the school-supply section, giving each other tattoos with black pens, then changing our minds, trying to rub them off, red skin, no luck. To the makeup section, where Nadine swipes a tester of red lip gloss across my lips. "You're so pretty," she says.

When school starts, Nadine and I will be in grade seven, which will be our last year of elementary school, which means we will be the oldest. So maybe I should start wearing red lip gloss.

I look in a mirror: It looks like I ate raspberry jam. It kinda tastes like jam too.

Um. Maybe I won't get it after all.

We all meet up at the checkout counter. Each kid has picked something out: Nadine vanilla lip gloss, me some grape-flavored gum, Jen a newspaper, Megan a sniffle from the frozen foods section. And Mrs. Ando still has the clam chowder. Nadine flashes me a look, as if saying, *We're definitely eating at your house tonight.*

The cashier is a tall blond woman. She looks like a model, even in her red-and-white uniform. She slides each item through the scanner. *Beep. Beep beep.* The lip gloss, *beep*. She keeps looking at us kids, at Mrs. Ando, then back at us kids.

She asks, "Are these all yours?"

"No." Mrs. Ando laughs. "One isn't. Guess which it is."

The cashier points to Megan, whose skin is a lot lighter than the rest of ours. Mrs. Ando shakes her head and lightly places her hand on my head. "It's this one."

We jump out of the minivan as soon as Mrs. Ando pulls into the carport. We run down the driveway. Nadine grabs my hand.

"Where are you going?" Mrs. Ando asks.

"Fraaaaaance," Nadine hollers back.

"Are you having dinner over there?"

"Yeaaaaaaaah," we sing.

There are six houses in our cul-de-sac. Six different houses, in six different colors, which have probably changed colors six different times: peach yellow blue green rose white.

My house is light brown, like a paper bag. And we have the largest front yard in the cul-de-sac, perfect for summer sprinkler run-throughs. There is the Cortes house, which is dark brown with caramel garage doors, like a chocolate bar. Then it's the Chin house, which used to be Marty's—it's the exact same green as Green Timbers Forest, our favorite place to play hide-and-seek, a few blocks beyond the cul-de-sac. The baby yellow Singh house, then the lighter green Koffmann house (green tea ice cream), and finally, behind us, the prettiest house of all . . .

The Ando house. It's a bluish-gray color and sometimes, when it's about to rain, you can't tell the difference between the house and the sky. It has two big front windows that look like two big eyes staring back at you. And when it does rain, the water slides down the glass, like tears; it's so pretty. And through these windows, you can almost always see everything the family does, especially at night, when the blue flicker of the television makes dancing shadows glow.

We stop and look both ways before crossing the

street. There never are any cars. It is a cul-de-sac, after all. But we look, or at least make it look like we're looking, and dart across the circle of cement like mice on a kitchen floor. I hold my breath as we cross.

Nadine and I are sitting crossed-legged on my bedroom floor, chewing grape gum and making friendship bracelets for each other, weaving our favorite colors together. Pink is hers, purple is mine.

My ten-year-old brother, James, comes in to watch. The smell of bulgogi swirls up the staircase, into my room, and up our noses. This smell of garlic and sweet soy sauce means "Go downstairs."

Standing at the top of the staircase, I hear familiar sounds. I can tell that Auntie Moon and Uncle Dong are over because Mom's speaking louder. It's like her volume goes up or something when she speaks Korean.

"Hello, Sara!" Auntie Moon says. I love Auntie Moon's face. It glows, like a moon. But I think that's just her moisturizer or whatever.

She and my uncle, who aren't exactly my aunt and uncle, are sitting on the wooden stools that surround the kitchen island, watching my mother wrestle with opening a glass jar, throwing her head back, laughing loudly, the way she always does when we have people over for dinner. Dad is home early from work and quietly circles them, pouring red wine. Finally, Mom releases the jar's strong smell: kimchi.

Nadine watches Mom.

"Your mother is the most beautiful woman I know," Nadine once told me.

Mom stands at five foot four. She is thin, size 4, she once told me, which is weird because I'm a size 14 . . . but I guess that's kids' sizing. Her face is the shape of a flattened heart, with brown eyes, a small nose, and full lips, the only plump thing on her body. She never wears any makeup, except a deep red lipstick, two rose petals on her face. And it never comes off. Even when she eats, even when my dad kisses her, even at bedtime when she comes in my room to say good night.

"Sara Smith, did you practice piano today?" She furrows her brow, like she's actually saying, "Get your act together."

"Tomorrow. I promise," I say. Her brow irons out a bit.

In the frying pan: The meat sizzles louder, then softer, depending on how my mother's chopsticks slide across. Mom rips pieces of lettuce (water droplets fly!) and stacks each thin, crisp leaf on top of the others on a paper towel. Finally, the rice cooker's red light turns off, giving us the go-ahead.

"Okay, everyone." Mom laughs. "Buffet-style."

Though we've done this a million times, I show

Nadine how to hold the lettuce in her palm, spread hot rice on it, plop a few pieces of bulgogi on top, wrap it, and pop it in her mouth. "It's called ssam," I explain. We do this over and over again, and our mouths love the cold of the lettuce, the warmth of the rice, and the saltiness of the meat. And Nadine and I are glad that we decided to eat on this side of the street tonight.

I was just a year old when I first met Nadine Ando. We were the first families to move into the cul-de-sac. My parents were pushing my stroller down the driveway to take me to the edge of Green Timbers Forest to pick some blackberries because my dad wanted to make a pie. Mr. and Mrs. Ando were doing the same, carrying ice cream buckets and pushing Nadine's stroller. Her younger sister, Jen, then only a few months old, was strapped to Mr. Ando's chest. Mom said me and Nadine wouldn't stop looking at each other. "It was like seeing your reflection in a mirror," she said. "Right down to the mole above your lip." And for a long time, I thought the way we and our siblings looked was totally normal. I think it's because up until I was, like, five or something, I truly believed everyone everywhere had one Asian parent and one white parent.

2

I AM FIVE years old.

Every morning, I am so happy to wake up. I think, *I can't wait to play, I love everything.* It's summer. I get up and put my bathing suit on right away, rush downstairs, and eat a bowl of cereal. Then just as I'm finishing my bowl, the door opens and Nadine comes running in, barefoot, wearing her bathing suit, a pink one with ruffles around the tummy, like a tutu. She's growing out of it a bit so you see her nipples. It's so funny. I shouldn't laugh, though, because mine is small too; it goes up my bum.

Things we do: fill buckets with water, drown worms in them, spray the banana slide, slide down it, run through the sprinkler, and then do cartwheels through the sprinkler.

We come in for lunch, and then go back out until it's dark outside. It gets pretty cold sometimes and we shake but we just hold each other for a while, warm up, and then run around for a bit longer.

I climb up onto the piano bench and play for Nadine all the songs I learned in my new piano class: "Hot Cross Buns," "Itsy-Bitsy Spider," "Twinkle, Twinkle, Little Star." She dances to everything so I play "Old MacDonald Had a Farm" and she walks around like a chicken, haha!

We knock on Marty's door. Marty opens it. He and his wife said whenever we want an ice cream cone all we have to do is knock on their door. We like Marty because he isn't old like our parents and understands us and our need for ice cream and goes away and comes back with one cone for each of us: Nadine and me. Sometimes we knock on his door four times a day.

Nadine and I slam her bedroom door closed because we don't want Jen to come in and play with us. We say, "If you tell on us, we won't play with you ever again." We say, "Shut up, you stupid baby." I say, "I won't play with you if you don't shut up."

And with this, Jen stops. She'll do anything just to play with us.

At lunch, while eating mac 'n' cheese (with a squirt of ketchup), I tell Nadine where I'm going.

"Korea," I say. "It's a place."

Nadine: "Where is it?"

Mrs. Ando, in the living room: "It's near Japan!" She walks in carrying Jen on her hip. "It's where Ojisan and Obasan are from!"

Before I have to leave, Nadine says, "Say hi to Japan for me." And then out of nowhere Jen starts crying. And then Nadine looks at Jen and starts crying. And then I look at Nadine and start crying. And we don't know how it happened but now we are all crying on the living room floor and can't stop. Mrs. Ando calls my house and Mom comes to take me home.

Halfway down the driveway, I hear music coming through the Andos' living room window. The Andos are playing "Sara" by Fleetwood Mac on their parents' cool record player. *She misses me already,* I think. I don't want to go, I don't. I don't want to be anywhere but with Nadine. But I cross the street anyway to go to Korea.

In the airplane, when Mom says it's time, I say: "Hi, Japan."

I love Halmonie. She is small and wrinkly and kind of smells like Mom and I don't understand what she says to me, but all my brother and I do is lie on her heated floor with her arms around us, watching cartoons on the

American army channel. I think, *I could lie here forever, I really could.*

I love Halmonie's food. It makes my tongue tingle. I eat a full bowl of rice at every meal and everyone pinches me and calls me tong tong, chubby. We eat dinner at breakfast. Rice, fish, vegetables, kimchi.

I teach Halmonie how to say "Shut up." She says it over and over and over again, and she knows that it's not nice to say and we both laugh, and Mom gives us a look, but then laughs too and lets us have our fun.

My aunts take my brother and me around to the shops and we point to something that we like in the window and they buy it for us right away. I wonder why they are so good to me, why they love me so much even though I never see them.

My relatives gather around me, everyone says, she's so pretty, she looks so western. Later, Mom tells me that they are saying how lucky I am that my eyes are so big, how I look like my dad. Though I feel sad because I don't want to look like my dad. He's a boy. I want to look like my mom.

There are so many uncles and aunties in Korea. My mom tells me to call all these people uncle and auntie and big sister and big brother, and I wonder if everyone in Korea is family.

Halmonie gives me some chicken feed. I go outside with her and she lets me throw the seeds on the ground.

The chickens are in their little house. Halmonie goes back inside and I feel like I'm the only thing outside, alone. But then big huge rats come out from underneath the little house instead, eating all the food. They go back under just as the chickens come out looking for food. The rats stole the chickens' food. I wish I could say something to someone.

My uncle is playing with his dogs, telling them to lie down, to bark, to sit, all in Korean. I say the same, in English, but they don't understand. It's a funny thing that these dogs can only understand Korean. These are really Korean dogs.

We're on the bus and a white man sits near us. Mom whispers, "He's from Canada too, he's got a Canadian flag on his backpack, see?" I walk up to him and start talking to him to see if he lives near us, and he says he's from a different place, and he doesn't care.

Mom says we've only been in Korea a month, but I feel like it's been forever. Mom hands over the phone to me and it's Dad, and it bothers me that I don't quite remember what his eyes or his nose looks like.

I don't want to leave. I yell as Mom carries me to the car. "I don't want to leave Halmonie," I say, and Halmonie looks through the car window and nods her head and though she smiles, I know her now, I know she is sad too.

*

At home, the house looks different. I'm not sure if the carpet is darker or lighter than how I remember.

Dad says, "Nadine is here." I peek my head around the corner and see her standing in the hallway, unsure whether to come in or wait outside, and when we look at each other it's like we don't recognize each other anymore. But then we go to my room and we play and everything is just like the way it was before.

3

NADINE AND I are at my house, playing with Cookie, my hamster. We put him in his plastic ball and let him run around the downstairs of my house.

I got Cookie more than three years ago, in grade three, after my orthodontist appointment one day. This happened after spending most of the summer trying to convince Mom it was a good idea.

I remember how I begged: "Pleeeease, Mom. I've never had a pet before."

"Why do you want a rat? They are so dirty. I don't understand," she said.

Me: "It's not a rat. It's a hamster. They're small and cute and they don't have those long tails."

She actually looked slightly thoughtful. She said hesitantly, "Just how long are their tails?"

"No longer than a centimeter, I swear."

"And when will it die?"

"In two years, I promise."

It's now past the two-year death wish and my hamster is still going strong. He's almost four years old. I'm not kidding. He's even got gray hair and survived a stroke. But I think the reason my hamster has lived so long is because when I first got him, my mom was too freaked out to let him in the house so she banned the cage to the garage. Cookie spent the first year inhaling the fumes of Mom's stinky Chinese medicine that she cooks on a little camping stove in the middle of the garage.

In the garage at night:

The pot simmers on low. My hamster runs on his wheel. Then he gets off and goes into the middle of the cage. He stands up on his hind legs, sniffing the air and breathing in the medicine.

Slowly, my hamster becomes . . . Super Hamster.

Cookie is so smart. And getting more so with age. We put him in his plastic ball and he runs all around the house in it. But when we want him to appear, all I have to say is, "Cookie, come here!" And he does, a small plastic ball spinning toward us, his little teddy bear face inside.

On the weekends during the school year, while I do my homework, I put Cookie in my left koala slipper to sleep. I even lay down one of Mom's maxi pads just in case he pees. But he never does. He is the best hamster ever.

Anyway, since it's Friday night, it's sleepover night, at Nadine's house. But we are still at my house.

Nadine: "Can we eat here, then go to my house? My mom's making meat loaf." (For the record, I actually like her meat loaf. But I think you always like someone else's mom's food.)

"Okay," I say. "Let's eat here."

Mom, from downstairs: "I'll make you bibimbap!"

Us: "Hooray!"

In a bowl: Steamed white rice. Different kinds of namul on top: spinach, thinly sliced carrots, radish, spicy bean sprouts, mountain fernbrake, beef, and fried egg. I mush it all up: a rainbow in my bowl.

After dinner, we help Mom put everything away, and I watch Nadine stand at the sink to do the dishes with my mom. "You're so lucky," she once said. "I wish your mom was my mom." Which is funny, because I wish hers was mine. It's more fun at her house. Mrs. Ando is so relaxed, and we do whatever we want without her getting mad at us. Plus she's always making cookies. My mom is stricter, like Nadine's father. Nadine and I often think that my mom and her dad should be married and that my dad and her mom should be married instead. But it's good to have balance, I guess. A bit of both.

❁

Cookie will be sleeping over too. I grab the cage and we start walking across the street. It's dark outside and the streetlights cast a big spotlight on us and Cookie's cage, like we're movie stars. Or prisoners.

In Nadine's room:

We stay up late, lying on her bedroom floor in our sleeping bags and talking about what we're going to do the last few weeks of summer. Like go to Crescent Beach when the tide is out, play hide-and-seek in the forest, and research new looks in magazines for grade seven. I'm secretly excited for summer to be over. I can tell Nadine is too. We can't wait to be the oldest and rule the school. Hey. That rhymes.

Moonlight streams through the window, between the blinds, and onto our faces.

The shine of Nadine's retainer and my headgear match the shine of the wire on Cookie's cage. As Nadine sleeps beside me, a strand of hair is in her face, and I lightly brush it with my fingers and tuck it behind her ear.

In the mall, I buy a gold pendant in the shape of a heart that says *Best Friends*. You're supposed to break it in half and give half to your best friend and keep the other for yourself. I'm going to wait for the right moment to give Nadine half of the heart.

I'm waiting for her to finish her ballet class.

I buy two chocolate bars from the vending machine, one for me and one for Nadine. But I eat mine right away, I can't wait.

Through the big glass window: A wooden floor that stretches under pink satin slippers, and when you look up, there is Nadine, in her pink bodysuit with her black hair coiled on top of her head, and her leg stretched out further than the rest.

After, when she's walking out with her pink bag over her shoulder, I give her her chocolate bar, already partially unwrapped for her convenience. She takes a huge bite and puts her arm around me and we walk down the hall and out the door together.

I love Nadine Ando. I love the way she spreads peanut butter perfectly on bread for me after school without making the bread tear underneath, and how she always smells like vanilla lip gloss because she applies it, like, every ten minutes, and how she walks with her feet slightly pointed outward kinda like a duck because she's permanently stuck in first position.

It's only ever been Nadine and me, her family and mine. And though we live in separate houses and have separate names, it's never really felt like we have separate lives. It's the way my shoes line up at their front door, the way my favorite snack sits on their kitchen table after school, the way I can still smell her house on my clothes when I come home. Sometimes, because we are together so much, it feels like we are one person. And I don't think this will ever change.

4

ONE DAY, in the grocery store parking lot:

He has blond hair and is helping his even blonder mother load grocery bags into the back of their green minivan. We are following our blond mother (Mrs. Ando) to the red minivan. Our vans are parked across from each other.

He's about half a head shorter than me and is wearing a Toronto Maple Leafs hockey jersey. His cheeks are pink, as though someone smeared strawberry yogurt on them with a butter knife. Something about him reminds me of someone. Maybe he was on TV? He jumps up to pull the trunk door down, his flip-flops making a squelchy sound. He smiles at us quickly. I smile back with my lips closed because I don't like people seeing my braces. Then he disappears into the van and they take off.

I don't think too much of it, but Jen is standing there shaking her fist in the air. "A Maple Leafs jersey?! Does he want to get killed here?" she says.

Mrs. Ando: "Jen, can you take the cart back?"

When we get home, Jen runs upstairs and immediately puts on her Vancouver Canucks jersey.

After that, she wears it for a week straight, hoping she'll run into him again.

Jen Ando. Okay, before we go on, there's some more you should know about Jen Ando. Besides being probably the smartest person any of us have ever met, even though she's a whole year younger than me, you gotta know how much she's into this whole save-the-world thing. So much so that some nights she can't even sleep because she's that worried about the situation in the Middle East. I guess that's what happens when your favorite TV show is the six o'clock news. When there was an earthquake in California, Jen wore her red bicycle helmet to bed every night, but her parents snuck in and took it off her so she wouldn't choke to death. Yup, that's my girl. And one time, at recess, when Scarlett Davies asked her if she wanted to try her eyeliner, Jen just said: "No. 'Cause I'd look like you." Booya. I liked her for that, too.

After dinner, James and I play with the Ando sisters in the patch of Green Timbers Forest that is closest to our cul-de-sac. It's our favorite place to play. We keep saying we are going to explore the forest further to make a fort, but we haven't done it yet. The forest stretches across a highway and many more streets and Dad once said it was over five hundred acres. It's kinda strange to think how there is this massive forest in the middle of all these cul-de-sacs and houses and basketball hoops.

Soft beams of evening sunlight come down through the trees at different places, highlighting certain parts of the forest: some leaves, bark, and moss. The dirt feels like sponge under my feet.

I'm It.

And I run down the trail, whip around stumps, crawl under fallen trunks, looking.

Where is everyone?

"Guys?"

I get really quiet. I hear someone behind a blackberry bush. It's Nadine. She's making noises I recognize. I think she's eating blackberries.

"Boo!"

She just looks up, her mouth stained purple. "These are pretty good, actually. Have some."

James and Jen emerge from the trees and we all start picking and eating the berries and totally forget about who's It and what game we are playing because of the sweet berry bombs exploding in our mouths.

Then everything around us becomes a shade darker. It's funny how it suddenly happens like that.

"Maybe we should go back. It's getting pretty dark," Nadine says.

In single file, with Nadine leading, we poke out of the dark forest like a needle, onto the street and into our cul-de-sac.

We look up: The moon has come out. We run in different directions for a while, seeing who the moon follows.

"Look! It's following me!" Nadine says.

"No, it's after me!" I say.

"You're all liars! It's coming this way!" says Jen.

"Look at how close it is!" says James. "It's, like, right here."

As though through a microphone, Mom's voice: "Get inside now!"

That night, as I lie in bed and watch the moon fill up the entire window, like a giant marble glowing at me, I think about how school is starting soon. I am so so so excited. I know, I know, it's weird.

Nadine and I are sort of known in school. People call us "the twins" even though Nadine is six months older and three inches taller. Plus, her hair is darker, longer, and shinier. Plus, she's skinnier. I'm a little rounder, everywhere. "But boys look at you more," she says. "You have boobs."

This year, we are going to have Monsieur Tanguay. He's the teacher everyone makes fun of. He's pretty old, like forty, and drives this funny old Volvo and wears tennis clothes to class. Anyway, apparently (this is what someone told me), the thing to do in grade seven is to order pizza to his house and then prank-call him at, like, one in the morning and burp repeatedly on his answering machine. I can't wait.

NADINE AND I are riding our bikes around the cul-de-sac. Round and round and round, pink streamers on Nadine's handlebars floating back and weaving into her hair, looking like highlights.

Our green minivan is backing out of the driveway and Dad rolls down the window and James leans toward us. "Wanna come to my baseball game?"

"I don't like baseball, sorry," I say.

Dad: "If you come, we can go to that hamburger joint on the highway you like."

Me, Nadine: "Okay!"

We hop in the van. Nadine doesn't bother to tell her mom because she'll figure it out eventually.

At the game:

Next up to bat on my brother's team is that blond kid from the parking lot. His hair kind of sticks out from under his helmet, like golden wings. He hits the ball to left field and makes it to second base.

Now it's James's turn. He's the smallest kid on the team and the only one wearing glasses. The metal bat looks kind of heavy for him.

The pitcher squints at my brother in the most evil way and violently throws the ball. But James remains steady and . . . BAM! Over the fence and into the preschool playground! Home run! The blond boy crosses home plate and James touches all the bases. Everyone rushes to my brother to hug him and carry him like a champ.

James and Dad slowly pack up equipment, chatting to everyone, taking for-friggin'-ever. I make Nadine walk to the car with me, thinking it'll make things move faster, but it doesn't. We just stand there locked out of the car. I'm so hungry for hamburgers, I think I'll die. Please, everyone just hurry up. Nadine knows how I get and says, "Here, have some," and hands me her water bottle. I quickly take a swig, hoping not to give her any backwash, but I know it's okay, she doesn't really care if I do.

6

I'M AT THE bank with Mom, who is waiting in line, staring at an empty doughnut box at the customer service table, when someone comes up behind me and says, "Crap."

It's Nadine.

It's strange to see your best friend somewhere in public by chance, like she's just a random person you ran into and not someone you're always with every second of the day.

"Hi," I say, stunned that she kind of swore.

"I really wanted one," she says. "Want a coffee?" She pulls two Styrofoam cups from a tall stack.

"Sure?" I say. "I didn't know you drank coffee."

"I've always liked coffee, since I was really little, actually. I take a few sips from my dad's cup when he isn't looking. I think the trick is to put a lot of cream and sugar in it like this to make it taste good. Apparently it suppresses your appetite too."

"I thought it just made you hyper."

"That too. Here." She hands it to me and I take a sip of my first cup of coffee ever.

The next morning:

I love the color of coffee with cream in it. It looks like caramel.

"Since when do you drink coffee?" Dad asks.

"I don't know," I say. "Haven't I always liked coffee?"

"Coffee Crisp, maybe."

Kiss on his cheek. "I'm going to the mall with Nadine," I say.

"Need a ride?" he asks.

For some reason, when Dad drives, it's better than when anyone else does. He's patient and calm and he makes the most beautiful curves around corners. And I swear if there were a pencil dragging behind the car and someone were looking down from above, the most intricate drawing would appear.

Nadine and I are sitting on the floor of the pharmacy, flipping through fashion magazines. I'm looking for a dress for grade seven prom. It's going to be a big deal, graduating from elementary school, you know. I'm super excited.

Nadine should be looking at dresses. Instead, she reads a teen magazine and can't stop laughing. She's reading the embarrassing stories section. I remind her why we're here, on the floor, with all these magazines.

"Sara, it's only elementary school," Nadine says. "Wait till grade twelve prom. That will be way more exciting."

I quickly flip through *Vogue*. Different perfumes waft into the air.

"That magazine kind of stinks," she says.

One year, I think we were eight or nine, Nadine and I were in my garage looking for roller skates or a hula hoop or something, when we found an old packet of forget-me-not seeds on a shelf behind a toolbox. The packet was stained, as though it had been soaked in tea for a couple of years and left to dry out for a couple more, so we were unsure if they were any good. But once we stepped outside, onto the small patch of grass between the garage and the gate, Nadine suddenly ripped open the packet with her teeth and threw the seeds on the ground in one motion. We laughed. I mean, whatever, right? Months passed, possibly even years, then one morning, when my dad was out of town for work or something and I had to drag the garbage bins out of the garage across that patch of grass, I saw them: little blue flowers everywhere. It was such a surprise.

But the truth is, that patch of earth was changing all along, we just couldn't see it. Once Nadine threw the seeds onto the grass, the seeds found a way to germinate because of the right temperature, amount of water, oxygen, and light. All these things had to come together for the flowers to bloom.

7

I'M IN THE washroom. Mom, downstairs, yells: "Sara! Telephone. Sara! Sara! Sara!"

"I hear you! I hear you! I hear you! Jeez," I yell. I run to my parents' bedroom. Belly flop on the bed. I know who it is because only one person ever calls me.

"Hello?" I ask.

"Is your mom mad at me?" Nadine asks.

"No, she's just kind of louder today," I say.

"I see." She laughs.

"What's up?"

"You're the one who called me. I'm just calling you back."

"Right." I laugh. "I forgot what I was going to say. . . . Oh yes! So my brother and his baseball team are going to the movies tonight, you want to go? We don't have to sit with them if we don't want to."

"Oh, cool. Okay. Jen may want to come too."

"Sure. My dad can drive us," I say.

"Great. Also, I have something to tell you, something crazy."

"Cool. Well, I gotta go practice piano now. Bye."

I hang up and roll over, staring up at the ceiling. All the white bumps look like some sort of skin disease. I think about a couple of random things, like how I should ask Mom to give me money for popcorn and pop and whether I should clean Cookie's cage today or tomorrow. I decide on tomorrow and go downstairs to practice piano for a bit.

Later, the four of us (me, Nadine, Jen, and James) are sitting in the minivan waiting for Dad to get in to drive us. I'm wearing a navy sundress with yellow flowers on it and a jean jacket. Nadine is basically wearing what she wore to dance class: a pink bodysuit, but with jeans over it. Jen is wearing her Vancouver Canucks hockey jersey with cycling shorts, which are too short, so it looks like she is wearing the jersey as a dress, even though she wouldn't be caught dead in one.

8

IN THE MOVIE THEATER:

We all sit in a row. Us kids from the cul-de-sac sit together: Nadine, me, Jen, James, then it's a bunch of the boys from the baseball team, including that boy. Thirteen of us in a long line.

My brother says his name is Daniel Monroe and he just moved here from Toronto. He's the same age as James and lives on the other side of Green Timbers Forest, like way over on the other side of Fraser Highway and down some.

Anyway, I bought the biggest bag of popcorn and the largest pop with the money Mom gave me. I just have to make sure I share with my brother, which I will, but I plan to mainly share with Nadine. There are two straws in the pop: one pushed down to be shorter (for me), the other pulled up to be taller (for Nadine).

Honestly, Nadine and I aren't really watching the movie much. Once we eat as much popcorn as we can, we are mainly concerned about sending the big bag of popcorn down the line and getting it back. Sending it down and getting it back. Every time Daniel gets it, he gives us a thumbs-up. Anyway, we do this the whole movie until it's gone. I also pass my pop to James a bunch (he knows which straw to use), even though he already had a massive pop to himself, and will totally have an accident tonight. Anyway, Nadine and I just giggle and point at the couple making out in front of us. It is kind of funny but super awkward. They are definitely missing the movie, but then again, I guess so are we.

9

THE LAST STRETCH of summer! Things I do with the Andos: run through the sprinklers, slide down the banana slide, wear bathing suits all day, every day, chase after the ice cream truck, drink out of the garden hose, have sleepovers every single night, play hide-and-seek until the sun goes down . . . and, of course, ride bikes to the corner store. Me, James, and the Ando sisters.

It's only about a five-minute bike ride down the road by the forest to the corner store, but it always seems so far away. It's in a little strip mall with a Chinese-takeout place, a laundromat, a liquor store, and a pub. Metal-heads with long hair wearing Judas Priest shirts usually hang around outside the pub, but Mrs. Ando told us never to make eye contact with them. I'm not sure if it's because she thinks they're dangerous or if it's because she's not into heavy metal.

There is everything any kid could want at the cor-ner store: ChapStick, candy, Wite-Out. We all wander around the store separately for a bit, then meet up at the Slurpee machines, which always look like mini washing machines to me. I pull a lever and watch the neon blue slush coil down perfectly. If I have one true talent in life, it's filling up Slurpee cups. I'm really good at it, and plus, the younger ones always make a mess when they try. I give Jen and James each a full cup. Then I pull the lever down on a different machine and cherry-red icy goodness oozes out. We go to pay at the counter. Nadine also buys a whole bag of sour keys candy and gives one to everyone.

With our red-and-blue stained mouths open, we bike home, E.T.-style.

10

NADINE CALLS. James and I both answer (James in the kitchen; me across my bed, in my room): "James, get off the phone." (He doesn't.)

Nadine: "Pleeeease, Sara, I need your help buying new clothes for school. I don't know what to wear."

Me: "Okay, we can go now. My dad can drive us."

James: "Hey, can I come?"

Me: "Get off!!"

Nadine: "Of course you can come, James."

Dad drops us off at the entrance to the department store, which is annoying because it's on the far side of the mall where there are no cool shops so we have to basically walk through the entire mall to get where we want to go. But I think he just drops us off here because he likes to avoid as many left-hand turns as possible.

Anyway, I lead Nadine and James through the lingerie section (awkward with James there), up the escalators, through the makeup section (stop for two squirts of my favorite perfume in my hair), and finally we are in the mall.

We walk through the mall's long corridor, which goes over 104th like a bridge, connecting the two parts of the mall. There are mirrors along the walls and as we walk I watch our reflection and think Nadine and I kind of look good together, like how ice-skating pairs do, except we're both girls.

Nadine stops and points at the chocolate store where they have my favorite hedgehog chocolates that taste like Nutella. "Can I buy you guys an ice cream? My mom gave me money."

Nadine gets a strawberry ice cream cone ("My favorite fruit," she says), and I get pralines and cream ("My grandmother loved it; she died before I was born," I say), and James gets bubble gum ("I just like gum," he says).

We sit on wooden bench: Nadine, me, and James. As we lick away, and as I watch people pass by with their shopping bags, and see a toddler trying to keep up, I have this weird feeling we've done this before together, or will again in the future, or that it will be the last time.

"So what's our plan?" I say. "I was thinking today we should focus on buying your clothes, mainly because I forgot to get money from my mom."

Nadine is silent for a minute. Then she says, "I'm really worried about the upcoming school year. I think it's going to be hard."

"I don't know if it'll be hard, but I do know that if we don't have anything new to wear, it'll be a disaster. I think we should wear matching outfits, but different colors. Just for the first day of school, of course. It'll be funny. We are 'the twins,' after all."

"Maybe," she says quietly. "I'm actually not really looking forward to school starting. I wish summer would last forever."

"School will be fine. It always is. We have each other. Plus, we still have a few weeks of summer left, Nadine. So all we need to worry about right now is getting you some new stylin' clothes."

James says, "Hey, wanna pitch the tent in the backyard tonight and have a sleepover?"

That night, after Nadine and I go into our separate homes for supper (spaghetti and meatballs for James and me, dunno what the Andos had), the doorbell rings and it's Nadine and Jen, with their camping equipment in a half circle at their feet, their black sleeping bags looking like big burnt marshmallows.

In the backyard, Nadine sets up the massive tent she brought over. She used to be a Girl Guide, before dancing took up all of her time and she had to quit. But she got a lot of badges. She can easily make a fire without matches and navigate by looking at the stars. When she opens the tent, it reminds me of an umbrella or a parachute.

James drags Mom's old golf bag out from the shed while Jen pulls small unripe apples from the trees. Nadine and I run into the house and upstairs to get Cookie's cage from my room.

From my bedroom window:

We watch James and Jen drive the apples into the neighbor's pool behind our house, *plop plop plop*, like rocks skipping on the ocean.

Later, in the dark:

Snug in our sleeping bags like worms, we all look up through the thin fabric of our tent at the stars. They are that bright.

James: "Some boys from my team want to camp in Green Timbers Forest before the end of the summer. Daniel says there is an open field somewhere in there. I bet we could see more stars there. We should do it."

Me: "We'll see. Let's talk about it another time."

Nadine: "Yes, time to sleep."

Everyone, separately, like dominoes, says, "Good night."

"Good night."

"Good night."

"Good night."

And with the faint smell of James's pee in the air (because he ate a lot of watermelon earlier) and the sound of Cookie running on his wheel, we all fall asleep together.

11

I HAVEN'T BEEN practicing piano as often as I should this summer.

When I practice, I don't really think about what I'm doing too much. It's not that I hate piano or that I'm bad at it, because I'm actually pretty good and come in first place in competitions and stuff. I just don't love it, you know, like the way Nadine loves dance. So when I practice, I let my fingers do the work and do my real, true favorite thing: daydream.

I think I like daydreaming because it gives me a break from it all. I usually have a general daydream that I keep going back to, to see what happens. This general daydream lasts for months, until I get a new one. For a while I had this great one about me living in Hawaii and scuba diving every day with the turtles. And all I ever wore was yellow and orange swimsuits, and I ate pineapples and mangoes and then wrote in my diary on the beach until sunset.

Sometimes I daydream about things that haven't

happened, but other times I dream about things that have already happened. They are more memories, I guess. Good memories.

We are all little.

Nadine and I are in preschool. It's our first day. We sit next to each other on the orange carpet; it smells like farts, I think because this boy in blue sweatpants keeps farting on it whenever we sit down. We sing, "Bonjour, mes amis, bonjour! Bonjour, mes amis, bonjour! Bonjour, mes amis, bonjour, mes amis, bonjour, mes amis, bonjour! Bonjour!" And I don't know what it means, but we sing it loudly, screaming almost, squeezing our eyes shut.

We run from the car to Bear Creek Park, straight for the swings, our favorite. We pump and pump and swing so high that it feels like we might go over and around, like a gymnast on a bar. We slow down and jump off to see who can jump the furthest. It's always Nadine; I always get scared last moment and do a little hop. Then we go on the tire swing.

"But there is bird poo on it," I say.

"It's okay," she says. "It's dried up."

"Really?" I say. She nods.

I sit on it and swing. And she's right, it's totally fine.

After, we go on the teeter-totter and try to make each other pop, not poop, up to the sky.

KNOCK! KNOCK!

My brother and I open the door: It's the Ando sisters, all three little faces staring at us.

"There's a rainbow in the sky!" they say. "There's a rainbow in the sky!"

And we look.

Arching over Surrey is the most BEAUTIFUL and SPARKLY and MAGICAL rainbow you ever saw. Like someone threw their crayons in the air and smudged them across the sky.

Mr. Ando has us all line up across the front lawn under the rainbow to take a picture. I sit closest to Nadine. She's my best friend.

I'm practicing piano and looking out the window—you know, the usual—and see the Andos' van pull into the carport. They all leap out of the doors in floppy straw hats and sunglasses, white-and-navy-striped beach bags over slightly burnt shoulders. Nadine's the last one to get out because she's lugging the big cooler. She stops for a moment as though she can hear me play and smiles before she goes inside.

12

ME: "You made this?"

Nadine: "Yeah. It took me four days."

We are both standing at my kitchen table on our tippy-toes, looking into a big cardboard box with its top cut off.

Inside is a super intricate multilevel hamster playground with stairs made out of Popsicle sticks and empty toilet paper rolls as slides. More empty rolls are scattered around as tunnels.

"My aunt helped me line the bottom part with linoleum," Nadine says. "So you can clean up his pee easier."

"It's amazing," I say.

"You think he'll like it?"

"One way to find out."

We are alone in my room (James is out with my dad) hovering over Cookie's cage. Nadine carefully pulls him out and snuggles him. She gently pets him with her index finger. "He's so cute," she says.

She goes nose to nose with Cookie for a second, and then looks up at me and kind of stares. Not with intensity, but with softness. "Sara, you know you're my best friend forever, right?"

"Of course."

I hear the front door open. James yells, "Whoa!! What is this thing?!" and Nadine says, "Maybe we should take Cookie downstairs."

She carries Cookie all the way downstairs cupped against her chest, then gently releases him into his new playground. He goes crazy exploring everything, and gets stuck in a toilet paper roll because he's kinda chubby. But it's all good, because we pull him out.

Suddenly Nadine says, "Shoot. What time is it? I have to go."

This reminds me of when we were little and Nadine was over playing and she wanted to go home but I wouldn't let her go. I would do everything to make her stay: cry, yell, bribe her ("You can play with my Cabbage Patch Kid if you stay"). All of this made her want to go home even more. Once I blocked the door and refused to let her by, and once I bit myself on the arm and yelled for my mom, saying she bit me even though she hadn't, but my mom knew me, how bad I could be, and I eventually was forced to let Nadine go. Like now.

"Okay," I say. "But we still need to figure out what to

wear the first day of school. I can come over tonight and we can discuss."

"Maybe. I'll get back to you. I have a couple of things to do first," she says, and leaves.

13

MOM'S BEST FRIEND, Ms. Cha, is here until school starts. "It's too hot to be in Korea right now," Mom says. Ms. Cha lived across the street from her when they were little.

Mom and Ms. Cha spend the whole night lying on a quilt on the living room floor. In the morning, I come down and find them sleeping next to each other.

I make them blueberry pancakes (Mom taught me how to lightly press the blueberries into the top of the pancake with my fingertips while it's cooking) and coffee (Dad taught me), and Mom and Ms. Cha sit at the dining room table and eat and start talking about what so-and-so is doing and why so-and-so is no longer talking to so-and-so. I look at Mom as though I'm disapproving of them gossiping so much and Mom says to me, "Sara, there are three things in life: food, sex, and talk about other people."

Umm . . . okay.

Anyway, they start talking about the Korean War.

"We fled early," Mom says. Her father pushed a bicycle from Seoul all the way to Busan, walking and taking the train every once in a while. She sat in the basket on the bike with her younger brother. Halmonie and Mom's older brother and sisters walked behind, holding hands.

Ms. Cha: "We fled late. We were so late we had to step over dead bodies that were piling up in the middle of the street."

Then they start making those dramatic serious faces that Mom and her friends make when they are around each other. Eyes getting small, then really big. Mouths in a straight line, then opening into a circle. Foreheads relaxing and then tightening, deep lines spreading across, then going away.

Mom remembers being on the roof of a train and getting off just before a tunnel. Then later they heard that everyone on the roof had died going through that tunnel. "We were so lucky," Mom says. For a long time after, she thought people rode on the top of trains instead of inside.

Mom says that once they made it to the south, to a village just outside Busan, they stayed with family there. She and her cousins went into the hills to play with matches and lit the hill on fire. "The entire village came out with brooms to beat the fire out." Mom and Ms. Cha's heads tilt back and they laugh, mouths pointing to the sky.

Mom remembers American soldiers handing out Hershey's chocolate bars. She says that the first thing she did when she moved to Canada was buy a Hershey's chocolate bar. "But it was disappointing," she says. "I remember it tasting a lot better back then."

When they went home, years later, they found their house destroyed. Same with Ms. Cha's house across the street. Mom's dad had to rebuild and it took years before things were even slightly normal again.

"Korea has such a sad history."

Ms. Cha nods.

"We were invaded by everyone all the time for thousands of years. China, even Japan invaded and occupied Korea. A lot. But the Japanese don't put it in their textbooks," Mom says. "They deny it."

She says that Koreans were the best potters ever. The Japanese didn't know how to do it. "So you know what they did?" She moves in closer. "They kidnapped Korean potters and brought them to the south of Japan to make pots."

I can't imagine Nadine a kidnapper. Mom doesn't know what she's talking about.

14

NADINE AND I are on my front lawn in our bikinis. Well, she is wearing a bikini, I'm wearing a one-piece. I'm lying down and Nadine is at my feet painting my toenails with paint-and-peel pink nail polish. The sprinkler is on and when it comes around, it just misses my head, leaving a few drops on my forehead and my lower lip.

Nadine looks at me over her mom's tortoiseshell sunglasses and says, "I have to tell you something. I've been meaning to tell you for a while."

"Yeah, what?"

"I'm going to high school," she says nervously.

"Uh . . . yeah, me too," I say. "We all are, eventually."

"No, I mean I'm going to high school, like, next week. Once school starts."

"What?"

"I'm skipping grade seven," she says quietly.

Her words punch me in the stomach. I can't breathe. I struggle to sit up. "What? Why?"

"I need to be . . . challenged," she says in the same low voice.

"Says who?"

"Mademoiselle Jestin, my parents . . . me."

"When did you decide?!"

"The last day of school," she says. She looks down, embarrassed.

My face is hot. I can't believe this. Her. "You've known all this time?!"

"I tried to tell you, but I couldn't find the right moment."

She stops painting my nails and crawls up as if I'm on a swing and she's going to spider me. Face to my face, her legs over my hips and sticking out on either side. She hugs me to calm me down and whispers, "Nothing's going to change, Sara. I promise."

15

I OPEN MY eyes. They are swollen and sore from crying. I'm on the couch in the family room. I guess I slept here last night. Wrapped in the TV blanket, empty cans of orange pop all around me.

I feel nothing inside, but my body feels a lot heavier. It's hard to move.

The TV turns on. Dad sits in front of my feet, at the edge of the couch, trying not to disturb me. A British news anchor is talking and I look up: pictures of fire in the desert.

"What's going on?" I ask.

Dad: "Sorry I woke you, but a war has broken out in the Middle East and the Americans have sent troops to fight. . . . What are you doing down here?"

"The world sucks," I say.

"Yes, it sometimes does. Pumpkin, are you okay?"

Dad has this way of always knowing when something is wrong. I look at him and right when I'm about to say something, my brother runs in the room and says, "Wanna go to the pool?"

The dark changing room smells of wet cement and pee. I step into my damp bathing suit, tiptoeing over clumps of hair on the floor until I'm outside on the pool's deck, under the sun, blinded.

We jump in the shallow end and start tossing a yellow plastic ball back and forth, back and forth, and sometimes, when it's up in the air, it looks like there are two suns in the sky, for a moment, and after a while, I get tired, and randomly ditch the game and drop the ball in front of me and float away toward the deep end, hearing my brother yell, "Hey! Come back!"

For a while, I stare straight at the sun, then I flip over on my stomach so my face is underwater and close my eyes. All I see: white circles the size of the sun dancing around in the darkness behind my eyelids.

I sink down to the bottom of the pool and let out the biggest scream. Then I start to cry. This is where these kinds of cries belong, below the surface, where no one can hear.

I can't believe she knew all along and kept it from me and she even made me help her buy new clothes for high school, she betrayed me, she betrayed me. And all those times we were playing together and running through sprinklers she knew—she knew she was going to hurt me and leave me. Why is she skipping a grade in the first place? I mean, sure she's smart, but she's not the smartest person ever to have lived, and she's not that much smarter than me; okay, maybe just by a bit. She says she needs to be challenged in school, but since when is school more important than friends and more important than best friends? I don't know what I'm going to do without her; she's the best and she is leaving me.

When I come up, the water drips down my face and mixes with the tears and nobody knows, not even James, that I've been crying. Except for the fact that my eyes are red. But then again, that could just be the chlorine.

16

AT MY BROTHER'S baseball game. Alone. I mean, I'm with my dad, Mom, and Ms. Cha, but not Nadine. So yeah, alone. I didn't want to come, but Mom forced me to go. "You need to get fresh air, Sara," she said. Probably because all I've been doing is staying at home, in my room, sleeping or crying. But she doesn't know that last part. So Mom forced me to change out of my pajamas and come to the game, and I guess it isn't so bad here because I'm wearing sunglasses so people can't see my red eyes and my dad buys me a hot dog, which I eat so quickly because I haven't eaten much in days.

I go to the concession stand to buy pop. They sell ice cream here too. Which reminds me of ice cream cake and my birthday party tomorrow. I completely forgot. I'm turning twelve. I start to panic, wondering if Nadine will still come tomorrow. I think she will. I haven't seen her or spoken to her in a day and a half, which is the longest I've not spoken to her ever, except when she's been away on vacation.

I look out at what's going on in front of me. Right, that.

It's the final inning. Two outs. Our team is at bat. Daniel is on second base and James is on first. Some redheaded kid named Vaughn comes to bat, nodding at both James and Daniel, as though saying, "I've got this one, guys." He hits it—BAM!—to left field, and Vaughn bolts to first and James bolts to second and Daniel bolts to third and I jump up cheering; what an exciting game, maybe we'll go to that burger joint to celebrate after; and now Daniel is passing third base, coming home, and James is following him but then halfway between third and home Daniel looks up into the bleachers to the right of me and pauses, I mean stops dead in his tracks—and he just stares.

The catcher has the ball now and Daniel finally clues in to this fact and turns around and scrambles back to third, and James sees this and freaks and scrambles back too, because Daniel is coming his way. Daniel barely makes it to third before the ball is thrown to the third baseman, but now James is stuck between third and Vaughn, who just passed second. They both sprint back, but James doesn't make it to second to beat the tag so he's OUT and they LOSE the game.

Awww, darn. Tough luck, boys. My heart goes out to them.

After the game:

I see Dad invite Daniel to the burger joint, but he shakes his head politely and motions that someone is coming to get him, like his mom. As we drive off, I watch him on the tire swing in the school playground, twisting the swing's chains and releasing them, spinning out of control.

First, I hear the phone ring. Then, I hear Mom and Dad whispering and I think Dad leaving the house. The door closes. I fall back asleep. Then the door opens again and I wake up. I hear Dad and two other people speaking. And there are more people speaking through a walkie-talkie.

I go into James's room and wake him up. He seems to know something is wrong too.

We lightly step downstairs in our thin summer pajamas and see Dad with two police officers in the living room, a man with a big belly and a woman with so many freckles on her face it's as though they are all connected to make one big tan. I don't know what is going on. Dad seems surprised to see us up but then says, "Kids, come sit on the sofa. You're not in trouble, don't worry. These officers may want to ask you a few questions about Daniel Monroe. He's missing."

I suddenly become really dizzy because what I just heard is so unexpected and doesn't make sense and James keeps repeating, "Dad, what do you mean?" over and over again, which makes me even more dizzy. The female officer says, "When Daniel's mom came to pick him up after the game, he was nowhere to be found, and no one has heard from him or seen him since."

They ask us about what happened at the baseball game, if we remember anything strange about the day. I am so confused and can't remember much. I say that I saw him spinning alone on the tire swing and they write this down in their notepads.

The next morning, we cancel my party, and I pretty much forget about my birthday all together. But we sit on the sofa and eat the ice cream cake Mom already bought while we watch the six o'clock news. . . .

A picture of Daniel in a powder blue baseball uniform, holding a bat over his shoulder, smiling at the camera. The kind of photo parents put on their fireplace mantel or under a banana magnet on the fridge. Blue eyes that have the same sparkle as the topaz ring my mom keeps in her jewelry box but never wears, and hair the same gold as the bracelet next to it.

"Look, it's his mom," James says.

She is on TV, standing at a podium next to a police officer. I only saw her once in the parking lot for a second. She is crying. She looks straight at the camera, asking whoever took her son to send him home. Then she starts talking directly to Daniel, saying things like, "It's okay, I'm not mad, come home and everything will be fine." It feels as though she is staring at me, through the screen, calling me to help.

It's so strange that people you love so much can be in your life one day and then the next . . . gone.

17

IT'S THE NIGHT before the first day of school and I haven't done a single thing to prepare for it.

Usually, Nadine and I lay out our newly purchased back-to-school clothes on our beds, go back and forth between our houses, and discuss and debate it forever, making sure we match, but not too much. But that did not happen this year. Mom bought me a few shirts and pairs of jeans, so I guess I'll have something to wear.

When I close my eyes and think about what tomorrow will actually look like without Nadine there, I can't see it. I still don't believe it's real. Maybe it was all a joke and she'll be there? Maybe she'll hate high school the first day and come back to our class the next?

This weird hope gives me enough energy to pick up some clothes off the floor, but not all of them, because a slightly messy room makes me feel less lonely.

I decide to focus on my desk—to organize and clean it. I sharpen pencils and stick them in a jam jar, erasers leaning against the side. Why do I always want to eat white erasers? Maybe because they kind of look like marshmallows or dduk. Anyway, I open a package of erasable pens and put them in the jar as well. This year, I'm going to start using erasable pens, no more pencils (except for math, maybe), because I've decided pencils are for kids. I throw out all the random pieces of paper in my desk that have been there forever (mainly old doodles and drawings) and place my *Bescherelle*, my French verb book, at the top right corner of the desk so I have access to look up verbs easily.

I will do well in school this year. I will. I promise myself this. Who knows, maybe I can skip a grade too. I did mostly get As last year, except for Bs in math and science. I mean, those are decent grades.

I open my window to keep me cold so I stay awake and alert. I sit down at my clean, perfect desk and open my *Bescherelle* and look at some verbs to refresh my memory since I haven't spoken any French all summer. I also flip to the index to look at new verbs. Cookie sleeps in the slipper at my feet.

Sacraliser. To make something sacred.

Mom comes in my room, eyes squinting like she just woke up, probably to go to the washroom.

"What are you doing still up? It's past midnight."

"I'm getting ready to study this year. I'll go to bed soon."

"Good girl. Kids in Korea stay up this late studying all the time," she says. "But don't forget to close your window. And lock it. Be careful."

I stay up for a while longer, then slide the window closed and crawl into bed. Tomorrow, I'll start working hard at school and be on my A game, for real. Tomorrow, everything will be better.

IT'S THE FIRST day of school and I can barely keep my eyes open. I'm standing around waiting for the bell to ring. Jen is skateboarding with Josh Weinstein and Ahmed Massad at the back of the parking lot. James runs alongside them as they glide, hoping they will let him go for a ride.

I should be more excited to be here. I usually get really bored by the end of the summer and love coming back to see everyone, but this year . . . I feel nothing. I draw a line in the gravel with the heel of my right shoe. Dust comes up. Cough.

Anyway, I'm just standing around, waiting for the bell to ring, watching the same old cars roll up with the same old faces popping out.

A red truck: Ricky Grant with a new haircut, a blond mushroom on his head.

A yellow van: Heather Wilson with lots of hair spray, her bangs in a kind of fan above her head.

A silver sports car: Scarlett Davies with three shades of purple on her eyelids, like butterfly wings splattered across her face.

Jen and I are in the same class, the grade six/seven split with Monsieur Tanguay. He writes something on the blackboard. His butt wiggles a bit when he does this.

Our first algebra question. And I don't know what is more important to look at: the numbers or the spaces in between the numbers. They both seem equally important. Sometimes the numbers are different, sometimes the spaces are different. But I'm not sure if the spaces are different on purpose or if this is just because Monsieur is sloppy. I'm not sure, and I'm too afraid to put up my hand and ask. I think I should be true to the spaces on the board and copy them just so in my notebook. They must be there for a reason.

I look around the class and realize that I may be the only one seeing the white spaces in between; everyone else sees the black numbers.

And I can't help but think: *Someone is missing in this class and nobody seems to notice.*

Recess. Finally. Everyone asks me where Nadine is and I say the same thing over and over again (she's skipped a grade, she's in high school now) and watch how they feel bad for me, especially the teachers, which is annoying because they are part of the reason this happened in the first place. They're the ones who thought she was smarter than everyone else, including me.

I go to the washroom and into the last stall, by the brick wall, and cry. When I come out, Jen is there. I can tell she notices that my eyes and nose are red.

"I'm getting a cold," I quickly say, and wash my hands.

"Let's walk around the soccer field and talk," she says. "Fresh air might make you feel better."

Walking around the field, I notice there are more lunch monitors than usual, keeping an eye on everyone. Volunteer parents, I think.

"I haven't been sleeping much," Jen says, dragging her feet along the grass, making roadrunner lines behind her. "I can't stop thinking about the situation in the Middle East, and of course, you know. Him."

"Him?" I say.

"Umm . . . *Daniel Monroe?* You know, that boy we know who went missing?"

"We didn't really know him. We never even talked to him."

"Still, we saw him. Someone was saying he was supposed to go to this school."

"He lived pretty far away, actually, and I think he was in another catchment."

"Oh. Still, though, to think that could happen here.

And you were there, at the game, it could have been you. I can't stop thinking about it."

"Yes, I still can't believe any of it is real," I say.

"Nadine is super upset by it."

"She is?"

"More than anyone."

I look up at the monkey bars. All the little kids swing and dangle and jump around. I kind of wish I could join them.

But no, I can't. I'm in grade seven. All we are supposed to do: walk and talk around the soccer field and stop to watch Scarlett do gymnastics.

I look at the grass: Scarlett does backflips and handsprings and cartwheels. All the boys gather to watch. At the end, she does this little bow; she can be a bit of a show-off that way.

I don't belong here, I think. I belong somewhere else, with someone else. This isn't right.

Jen and I are getting picked up by Mrs. Ando, the world's funniest driver. She is always doing a million things behind the wheel: putting her makeup on, writing things down in her day planner, searching through her briefcase for something. One morning, she brought in a bowl of cereal. Cornflakes. She actually managed to finish it, without spilling any milk.

When Mrs. Ando drives, we kids usually speak French, the advantage of being in the French immersion program. It's usually Nadine and me who do this. But this time:

"Mon Dieu," Jen starts.

Me: "On est trop jeune pour mourir!"

Mrs. Ando gives us a look through the rearview mirror and smiles with her light blue eyes.

"Good girls. Keep practicing your French," she says. No clue. They never had French immersion when she was a kid. The car behind us, *honk honk*. We are laughing so hard. It's the first time I've laughed in a while.

Mr. and Mrs. Ando own their own small business. They met in college their freshman year. Mrs. Ando often tells the story of how when they met, their eyeballs turned into hearts. "Love at first sight," she said. It was like a fairy tale.

Then Nadine was born. She was a pretty cute kid. You should see the pictures.

Nadine eating a vanilla ice cream cone with her left hand, and with her right, pulling her right leg way up to the point where you can almost see her underwear with tiny ice cream cones on them (for real).

Nadine in front of a birthday cake, her little face glowing from the two pink candles stuck into the frosting.

Nadine sleeping on the living room couch, a patch of sunlight across her cheek, her thumb in her mouth.

We approach Nadine's new school, the high school, and my stomach starts to feel weird.

Weird in the same way it once did when I went up a super fast elevator to visit Mom's friend and then suddenly it stopped. Or like that time I was on Uncle Bill's boat on Lake Ontario and my stomach moved in waves, crashing against things it shouldn't be crashing against, like my heart.

Anyway, *the high school*. It has brown bricks on the outside, which seems more fancy than the painted blue wood that is our school. It's five times bigger, too, because all the kids from the different elementary schools in the area end up there. I've been inside once before, for a piano recital. I remember the long halls lined with metal lockers. I bet Nadine has a locker now. With a lock that only she knows the combination to, and won't tell anyone, including me.

The bell rings and students explode out of the school. Everyone is so tall and some don't even look like kids, they're so grown up. The girls are wearing clothes so stylish, I wonder where they bought them because I never saw any of it at the mall.

Nadine jumps into the front seat, waves *bye!* to a

group of girls, and immediately flips open the vanity mirror, puts on a new lip gloss (it smells like watermelon . . . wait, not vanilla?), and gets ready for ballet class. I haven't seen her since last week when she told me she was skipping a grade, except through the window while practicing piano. I try to act like it's totally a normal thing to pick her up from an ENTIRELY DIFFERENT SCHOOL.

Me: "Hi!"

"Hello!" Nadine says back, in a slightly forced way.

And just like that, me and my best friend start to have our first fake and totally awkward conversation.

"So who were those girls?" I ask.

"They were a year ahead of us. Don't you remember them?"

"Not really."

Jen: "Never seen those girls in my life."

Nadine: "Hey, Sara, are you coming over?"

"Of course," I say.

"Great! I have a little homework to do but it should be fine."

Nadine suddenly turns around and looks at us and says, "Why are you guys sitting at the very back of the van?"

Jen laughs. "Because we are the badasses in the back."

Nadine looks straight ahead again, and in the vanity mirror, I think I see her sort of roll her eyes.

And with that slight eye movement, I realize I will have to try extra hard after school to make sure we remain best friends.

On a telephone pole outside my window: A MISSING sign for Daniel. The photo must be from last Christmas because there is a tree with a string of twinkling lights behind him. Clear masking tape holds the poster to the pole. Uneven and wrinkled. Nadine makes a noise, close to a cry.

And that's when I get the idea. I know what can bring us together.

19

AFTER SCHOOL, I'm in Nadine and Jen's room, where they share a bunk bed. Nadine has the bottom, Jen has the top. It used to be the other way around, but they switched it this year.

I'm digging through Nadine's side closet: Baby blue and baby pink clothes fly behind me like shooting stars.

Nadine: "You really don't have to do that."

She is sitting over her pale wooden desk, the exact color of the ballet studio's floor. She is doing her math homework: geometry. She rotates a compass in a slow twirl. She lays the pencil down.

"Thank you," she says. "It's really nice of you."

"That's what best friends are for," I say.

It takes me two hours to color-coordinate and fold everything and by the time I'm done I'm wearing her white leg warmers and pink headband, I don't know how or why, but she doesn't seem to care too much. I close the closet door and hang her satin pointe shoes on the little knob (a ribbon on a present). After, I sit on Nadine's bed, hoping she'll notice.

Nadine: "Don't you have homework?"

Me: "Not really."

Jen walks in: "Uh, yeah we do. We have a math quiz tomorrow."

Me: "It's so easy, it'll take me just a couple minutes to review. I can do it later. Anyway, we have another matter to discuss."

Nadine: "Oh. Like what?"

"Daniel. I think we should start our own investigation."

Jen is into it: "Yes! Great idea!"

"You think?" Nadine says.

Me: "The police haven't been able to find him and we know him, so I think we have an advantage."

Nadine: "We don't really know him that well. We sort of went to the movies with him once and didn't talk to him. Do you even remember having a conversation with him?"

"Yes, the day he disappeared, at the baseball game."

"You did?"

"Well, I don't know if I actually talked to him. But I was the last person to see him," I say.

Jen: "What Sara's point is, is that we know him more than the police do."

Nadine: "That's true, we do."

Me: "And we know our neighborhood better too."

"Very true." Nadine pauses, then says, "Okay. Let's do it."

I continue to lie on Nadine's bed and begin reading a teen magazine even though I'm not a teen, and then all of a sudden, Mrs. Ando is touching my shoulder, waking me up. I get up and she walks me home, because no kid is allowed to walk home alone after dark anymore, and I collapse on my bed and fall asleep still wearing Nadine's headband and leg warmers. My own clothing is scattered everywhere on the bed and on the floor, like friends.

The next day, I barely pass the math quiz. Barely.

It was just one test, though, and I still have the whole year to make it up, right? At least I think so.

20

IT'S FRIDAY NIGHT. I am practicing piano. (Yes, lame, I know.)

Through the window I see Nadine dragging out a trash bin alone, which I worry is kind of dangerous. She pauses and looks into the distance, to the forest. I try to play my sonata as beautifully as possibly for her and I think it's affecting her because she starts to sway from side to side in her pink jelly shoes and she looks happy for a moment. And my fingers hit every key with so much love for her that my last note is so soft you can barely hear it. I look over and she gives a little wave. I bow a bit. She slowly turns as though she can still hear the music, because she is still kind of swaying, and goes back inside.

Ring. Ring. I run to the phone. My sort of sticky bare feet make squeaky noises on the kitchen floor.

Me: "Hello?"

"It's me." (Nadine! Yes!) "Nice piano playing, by the way."

"Thanks."

"Turn on the news. Now."

I peek into the living room. Dad is already watching.

The screen shows a picture of an older man wearing a white T-shirt and jeans. He has familiar rosy cheeks.

Nadine: "It's Daniel's dad. The police say they want to locate him to ask him questions."

"So he took him?" I say.

"They say he's a person of interest. That doesn't necessarily mean he is a suspect, but . . ."

"Maybe."

"Exactly. It's so sad. Sometimes I can't sleep, thinking about the whole thing."

"Me too," I say. "Want to come over for a while?"

"Sleepover?"

"Yah."

"I'll be right there."

I unfold the low black table from Korea with pearlescent flowers and fish engraved on it. When Nadine arrives, we sit at it, cross-legged, drinking cold chocolate milk.

I pull out a notebook and we sketch out a plan to search through the forest.

I'm happy because we have a mission, something we share: We are going to find Daniel Monroe ourselves. I know it may seem like I'm using the disappearance of that poor kid as a ploy to keep my best friend around, but I never said I was a great person.

75

21

I'VE CALLED OUR first meeting about Daniel Monroe at our house, in our living room. James drags chairs from the dining room into the living room, forming two rows, all facing the front where there's a big map of Surrey that I drew on a flip chart using smelly felt markers. The trees smell like peppermint, the trunks like cinnamon, the baseball diamond like black licorice.

On the coffee table, James has lined up apple juice boxes like dominoes. He closes the French doors.

In attendance:

Me

Nadine

James

Jen

Megan (too little to understand but Nadine is baby-sitting)

I lead the meeting, standing in front of everyone. I point to the flip chart with some random ruler I found in the junk drawer in the kitchen and say, "There are three possibilities for what happened to Daniel."

Jen clears her throat. "Well, the obvious one is that he was kidnapped. Maybe by some crazed childless couple who wants a kid."

Jen (to me): "What else did you come up with?"

Me: "Well . . . Nadine and I think his dad could have kidnapped him."

James: "Why would his own dad kidnap him?"

Jen: "Maybe because of a custody battle. His dad could have just decided to nab him. It's super common."

Nadine: "I don't know if I think that anymore."

Me: "Yes, because, what we really think is . . . he could have run away. We think he is camping in Green Timbers Forest."

"Why the forest?" Jen says.

James catches on. "Because he told me he wanted to camp there before the summer was done! That's it! That's where he is!"

"Yes!" I say.

Nadine: "I'm sorry, I have to stop this."

What on earth is she doing?

"I talked to my mom about this meeting. We should be leaving this to the police. Plus, they probably have already checked the forest."

I can't believe her. I thought she wanted to find him

together. She decided all this without even talking to me? How dare she?

James: "But, Nadine, we know the forest really well. At least the area near here. We really have a chance to find him."

"That's right, Nadine," I say. "Remember how we said he might be in the forest?"

Nadine: "The idea that the whole country is looking for him and he's just pitched a tent in the forest is insane. I don't think so."

"But I thought you wanted to do something to find him," I say.

"I did, and I'm sorry. But it's irresponsible for us to take matters into our own hands. Let's leave it to the police. They know what they are doing." She looks at Jen and Megan and says, "Time to go home."

Jen: "But I don't want to go home."

"We have to finish our chores today. It's Saturday."

"Fine, whatever. But you're doing the toilets," Jen says.

Nadine takes Megan by the hand and puts her shoes on. Jen remains silent in an angry way and follows them. As they walk down the driveway, Nadine turns around and mouths, *I'm sorry. I'll call you later.*

She doesn't call me later. I think she had a ballet recital and a lot of homework. Or else she just forgot.

22

"THREE PEOPLE. Perfect number of people for dim sum," Mom says.

Around us, the hum of a Chinese restaurant. Dad, Mom, and I sit around a round table. James is at a friend's house, not like he really has any, but whatever, yeah.

This is actually Nadine's favorite place. No one loves dim sum as much as Nadine. "The dumplings look like magical edible jewels," she once said to me. She used to come with us here almost every month. But she didn't today. When I called this morning to ask, she said she had too much homework. I'm not sure if it's because of what happened yesterday, though I don't think I did anything wrong.

Crisp white linen lies smooth under cold ceramic bowls and long chopsticks. A teapot. Mom takes it and pours hot golden tea into three little cups on the table. Me, with two fingers, tap tap on the table, *Thank you.* Nadine taught me this. I have no idea where she learned it.

Women in black bow ties slowly push trolleys by our table. Mom either shakes her head no or nods yes, depending on what's on the cart. Mom can understand some Cantonese, though she never lets the women with the carts know this.

Mom nods, and with prongs the women quickly place wooden dishes on our table, *whoosh whoosh whoosh*, a stream of dim sum treats.

In one dish: three steamed pork buns. Mom gives one to each of us. We all use chopsticks; Dad's a pro. He can separate and slice and do the most amazing tricks and I swear he could even catch a fly with those things just like that guy in *The Karate Kid*. Nadine is really good too. I am so clumsy with mine. Mom says not to feel bad, she's not so good herself.

I poke a hole in the bun. It breathes out air, pork air. I manage to open the bun, revealing its orange insides. This is my favorite. It's sweet and salty all at the same time. After, I eat the white fluffy bun.

And then Mom nods her head for more. Siu mai look like underwater creatures, pink on the inside, wrinkly green on the outside. Sticky rice wrapped in banana leaves. I peel the leaf off and try to separate each piece of rice from the other; impossible. Mom eats chicken feet. Dad and I dare not touch.

We eat a million different kinds of dumplings with

different kinds of things inside. Mushrooms, vegetables, pork, shrimp. Dad eats all the shrimp ones; he can't help himself. The shrimp ones are Nadine's favorite too. She doesn't like meat much.

I go to the washroom and do what is a tradition for me and Nadine: Stop at the big fish tanks, which look like cubes of ocean stacked up to the ceiling. Each tank is a different underwater world. One with giant goldfish happily swimming around, another with slimy black snakefish slithering through, and one with a layer of crabs sleeping, a single crab crawling on top of them, until it finds a place to rest.

I suddenly get very sad.

"Time to go," Mom says behind me.

We walk down the stairs to the bakery underneath. I am so full. But I get the usual there, an egg tart, because it's just what I always get. And Dad gets a coconut bun because that's what he always gets. Nadine would get a sesame ball with red bean paste inside. If she were here.

This is what we used to do at least once a month. Drop James off at his friend's house, come to Chinatown with Nadine, eat dim sum, go downstairs afterward for some baked goods, go to a market to buy vegetables, then stop to see Mom's Chinese medicine doctor, George.

In the medicine store:

Buckets of dried roots and other brown things. It's

so stinky. I plug my nose while we're in there. All I can think: *Poor Cookie*. I can't believe he had to live with this smell while exiled to the garage.

We walk up and down the streets of Chinatown. Mom and Dad drift ahead and I try to catch up with them; I can't see them anymore, but I do see a blond boy in a blue jacket walking and I try to catch up to him but somehow he floats up and away in a sea of people with dark hair, and walking right in front of me is Nadine, she is here, in Chinatown, what are the odds, and I tap her on the shoulder and she turns around, and it's not her, it's a woman, looking at me, confused and kind of angry I touched her. I'm so scared.

Someone grabs my arm. It's Dad. He says, "Stay close."

I realize I'm crazy for hoping that Nadine and I are still forever best friends, like how we were before. I need to be realistic. I have to try my hardest to make sure we remain best after-school friends. This is my new goal.

23

SINCE IT'S A nice day, our moms miraculously let Jen, James, and me ride our bikes to school. I feel it's a little immature doing this; it's probably better to walk or be driven, but Jen and James really want to bike to school and I don't want to fight it, because I have bigger problems, so it's like what the heck, you know.

After a few blocks, I feel strange. Then I notice the constant hum of the same car engine for a while. "Guys, let's get moving," I say. "I think someone is following us."

We start pedaling as quickly as we can. I look at James and he's pedaling so hard he's standing up on his bike, lunging his face forward, chin out, thinking it'll make him go faster. We cut through a grassy field, just missing a ditch, down a path between two houses, and into another cul-de-sac.

We've lost them. Phew. We slowly start to bike out of a different cul-de-sac and down a different road to school. Then I hear the same engine. A van pulls up next to us, and in the window: Nadine. With Mrs. Ando driving. Megan in the backseat, in her car seat.

Nadine rolls down the window and leans back for Mrs. Ando to speak: "Sorry! I was following just in case! But I see that you're fine! Bye!"

Nadine says nothing, just leans forward to roll the window back up, nods hello (or good-bye?) as they speed off.

And I wonder, if Nadine didn't skip, would she be here, with us, riding bikes to school? She probably would be. Yes. Of course. But instead she's the person who leans back in her seat and says nothing to her (after-school) best friend.

At school, all I can think about is Nadine and how she is not here, sitting next to me, or in front of me, or behind me, like how we usually manipulate the sitting plan to our liking.

As I'm thinking all this, I write her name over and over again in the same spot on the top right corner of my notebook, but it's okay because it just looks like a scribble, so Monsieur won't think I'm crazy, just a little messy.

❀

In the bathroom, in the last stall just above the toilet paper, I write: *SS + NA BFFs 4ever*. I write it in pencil to feel less bad so someone can erase it away easily.

I always stand in the same place after school, waiting to get picked up. This is my little square of the sidewalk. I never leave it. It's a great square, outlined with dirt. There are straggly weeds that grow in its grooves. There is one particular weed that is quite large. I am holding a water bottle above it and . . .

"Did you just water that weed?" Jen is standing in front of me.

"Uh . . ." A car pulls up. "My mom's here," I say. "I have to go to my piano lesson."

24

IT'S SATURDAY AFTERNOON.

Dad and I are going to a matinee today. We used to go every week, just him and me, but we haven't gone in a while. I guess recently I've preferred to go to the movies with Nadine and have my dad drop us off a block away from the theater. I think also that everyone has stopped doing the things they enjoy since Daniel went missing.

Sometimes, randomly, say when Dad is driving me somewhere, I'll look at him and miss him and wish we hung out more, like before.

I grab his hand in the car. I haven't held his hands in years. They are so soft.

Everything Dad does is on the left. The way he votes, the way he tilts his head to the side when he's thinking. He's even left-handed.

In the theater:

The movie has already started and Dad is still outside in the lobby buying popcorn and pop. I kind of get worried that he won't be able to find me in the dark, and keep looking back over my shoulder, ignoring the previews.

Then I see a shadow move down the aisle. It's him. He sits next to me (in the aisle seat, I always save it for him).

I whisper, "How did you know I'd be on this side of the theater?"

"You like to sit on the left side of things," he says. "The couch, the movie theater."

We watch the movie. And it's about a man getting killed, leaving his grieving fiancée behind. Little does she know, though, that he is actually still there, in spirit form, watching her and protecting her as she tries to figure out who killed him. Their connection is so strong that they feel each other and even though one is alive and the other is a ghost, she senses his presence and love wherever she goes.

I want to know a love like this, but I know deep down that I will be forever alone because my best friend has left me. Things will never be the same and I will never find another friend so true and honest and pure in a way that matches all those parts of me that are true, honest, and pure. These are the real and the best parts of me, and she brought them out. So I have no choice but to do absolutely everything I can to turn things around and make her come back so I can be whole again.

Dad puts his (soft) hand on mine, which is resting on the cup holder. "Are you okay, sweetheart?"

I'm not, I'm not okay. And I want to tell him this, but when I open my mouth these words come out instead: "Yes, I'm fine. What a great movie. Thanks, Daddy."

25

SO . . . SOMEHOW someone found out I was the one who wrote that thing in the bathroom. I'm not sure who it was, but someone told a teacher and lo and behold, I'm sitting in the vice principal's office—not the actual principal's office, which to me is a hopeful sign. The only thing that worries me is that there is a police officer talking to the secretary.

A woman walks in the room and says, "I'm Ms. Lee, the new vice principal."

Ohhh. That's who she is. I mean, she wasn't teaching any classes I know of and she was always in the hall, smiling at everyone as they came in. Plus, she doesn't look like a teacher. She looks cooler, prettier, like she doesn't belong here but in New York City, in an art gallery, sipping red wine.

She sits down across from me and looks at me with the most neutral expression for what feels like an eternity. I shift a bit on her crinkled-leather brown couch.

"We know it was you who wrote on the bathroom wall. This is very serious. It's technically vandalism."

"I'm sorry," I say and look down at my feet, noticing my mismatched socks. I feel Ms. Lee's gaze on them too. "I won't do it again. I promise."

"I hope not. The punishment for school vandalism is suspension. But since it seems you've never done anything like this before, I'm willing to let you go with a warning. Do not do it again."

Phew. But I'm still not completely at ease. "So then why are the police here?" I ask.

"Oh, they patrol all schools in Surrey regularly. It's standard routine these days."

She looks through some papers on her desk and I scan her office for any clues of her life. There aren't any framed pictures of family, but there is a big bouquet of flowers: white lilies. Probably from her husband. Except she doesn't have a ring yet. Boyfriend?

She looks up, surprised I'm still there. She says, "You can go." And as I get up to leave she casually asks, "Things going well in class?"

"Actually, it's kind of boring," I say.

"How so?"

"It's so easy," I say. "I need to be challenged."

Her: "You're finding school too easy?"

Me: "Yes, I think I could probably skip a grade."

"Oh?"

The second bell rings.

"Yah. We have a math quiz; gonna crush it," I say.

I slip into my desk as Monsieur Tanguay starts writing a weird equation with the strange spaces in between again. I hate these desks because the chairs are attached to them and it's so tight, I can't push back. I need to get out of here. I need to be with the grown-ups, I need to be with Nadine in high school, and I'll do whatever it takes to make that happen. I can't stay here. I have to convince the school that I can to skip a grade too. I have to get out of elementary school forever.

26

I TOTALLY FAIL the quiz, by the way. Two out of ten.

At night, I can't sleep. I can't believe I failed that quiz. I've never failed anything before. How am I going to pull myself out of this and get back on track? Last year, I did super well in math, but maybe it's because Nadine helped me out a lot, explaining things to me.

Nadine.

I have to stop waiting around, hoping that Nadine will invite me over after school, because she hasn't, and I need to focus on myself and making myself better in all ways to be worthy of skipping a grade and going to high school early. If I do really well, maybe they will let me into high school for the next term, starting in January? It's a possibility. I have a few months to work my butt off to make it happen. I can do it. I can.

27

TONIGHT IS THE first school dance of the year. There actually wasn't going to be one this year, because members of the Parent Advisory Committee didn't want their kids out late, but Jen told me she heard that Ms. Lee told them it was important to keep some sense of normalcy in the community and school by continuing to support activities like the dance. Ms. Lee also assured the parents that there would be a lot of volunteers supervising and that the police would send a patrol unit to sit in the parking lot. But even though it was happening, I still didn't really want to go, not because I was afraid, but because I wanted to study.

This all changed when Jen called saying we should go, like together, she and I, and that it would be fun, and I appreciated Jen calling me and asking because I kinda felt forgotten by everyone. Then I heard Nadine yell in the background: "Come over. I'll do your hair!"

So, like that, I'm at the Andos'.

I sit on a chair and Nadine hovers above me. She puts her super massive hairbrush on top of my head and pulls it down, porcupines crawling lightly down my skull. Nobody brushes hair like Nadine. It's gentle and ticklish and sometimes hurts a bit, but in a good way. It's been a while since I've been in super close proximity to Nadine, other than sitting next to her in the car. And I don't know how long it's been since she's touched me, even though she is just touching me with a brush. I haven't been coming over after school like usual. Probably because I've been trying to study more. Probably because she hasn't invited me.

"You have such awesome hair," Nadine says. "I would, like, kill to have your hair. It's so wavy and has so much body. Mine is suuuuuuper straight."

Jen walks in wearing jeans. "Is this okay to wear?"

Me: "Yes. It's an elementary school dance. Who cares."

Nadine laughs a bit and I think, *This feels great*. It's like we are on the same page, equals. Things feel normal again. Until I realize she is helping me get ready for a dance she is not going to.

Nadine to Jen: "Hey, wouldn't you kill to have Sara's hair?"

"No. That's a little extreme," Jen says. "Definitely not worth twenty-five to life in prison."

Nadine continues, "Actually, Rachel has pretty cool hair too. Some of it is so blond, it's almost white."

Jen: "That's called albinism."

"Rachel? Who is Rachel?" I ask.

"She's a girl in my school. She's really pretty. Her hair is so long and blond. She even has highlights. *Natural* highlights."

Jen rolls her eyes. Nadine tells me to lie on Jen's bed and close my eyes.

"I'm going to pluck your eyebrows ever so slightly," she says. "They're a bit bushy."

Jen: "Seriously, Nadine? They're fine."

"No, it's okay," I say. "I want to."

I rest my head on Jen's pillow and close my eyes. I can feel Nadine breathing on my face, she's that close, then the cold metal of the tweezers touches my forehead and then RIP! RIP! RIP! RIP! RIP! I scream, "STOP!!"

I grab the tweezers from Nadine and run to the bathroom. I pull the rest of the stray hairs out myself, tears streaming down my cheek into the sink.

I look in the mirror. I made it worse. Half of one eyebrow has disappeared.

She did this on purpose, I think. She's done everything on purpose. Like how she made me go shopping with her for new clothes for her new school. Just to spite me. She's getting some sick pleasure from seeing me like this, hurting me like this.

I come out and Nadine and Jen are in the hall. Nadine and I just stand there looking at each other.

Jen says, "It looks fine, honestly."

"Your hair grows back so fast anyway," Nadine says. "And it'll be dark at the dance. No one will notice."

I walk past both of them angrily and go downstairs to put my shoes on.

In the school gym:

I am hypnotized by the blue and red flecks of lights from the disco ball as they dance along the walls and on people's cheeks. They calm me down and make me feel better.

The gym isn't that full. I'm guessing only sixty percent of the kids came. Mrs. Ando stayed to chaperone, which is kind of awkward if I decide to dance with a boy.

It's a slow song and all the boys dance with the girls at arm's length. Girls with their hands on the boys' shoulders; boys with their hands on girls' hips, rocking back and forth. I'm dancing with my friend Josh. Mrs. Ando drinks punch with Ms. Lee and some of the teachers and watches us. She waves hello when she sees me.

During the fast songs I don't know how to dance to the music so I just pull Jen aside and whisper in her ear, as if I have something important to say, but I don't, it's just because I don't know how to dance to fast songs. I do dance a bit with Jen and Josh but in a joking way, like monkeys or robots. Josh does the Running Man. It's pretty good.

It's another slow song. Jen goes off to talk to a teacher. Ricky Grant asks me to dance. Why does he want to dance with me? He's always flipping his eyelids at me, which really makes me mad because there is nothing I find more disgusting. In class, he taps me on the shoulder (he sits behind me), and I turn: It looks like there are earthworms on his eyelids. I fall for it every time.

As we dance, he presses himself up against my hip a bit. Eww. Whoa, what? I pull away and he becomes less weird.

While I dance with him, I close my eyes and try to imagine that I'm dancing with someone else, like a friend, like maybe Josh or something, or even Nadine, even though I'm kind of mad at her right now, but then I hear the lights go on and I open my eyes to see Ricky's face and the volleyball net against the wall and the primary-color lines on the floor and Mrs. Ando looking at me. The dance is over.

When we drive into the cul-de-sac, and Mrs. Ando pulls into my driveway to let me off first since it's so dark, I see Nadine looking at me through her bedroom window. But when she sees me, she just closes the blinds.

And while I was angry at her for plucking my eyebrows out, all I want is for her to open them again and wave hello.

I have to try harder.

28

MOM DRIVES US to piano lessons at Mrs. West's home in New Westminster. She lives in this super small white house with a green roof. It looks like something from a fairy tale, as though elves live in there, but it's only my six-foot-tall piano teacher and her grand piano.

Anyway, whenever it's my brother's turn, I go in the bathroom to look through her beauty stuff. She's got some really cool soaps that smell like fruit—apple, strawberry, and lemon. I don't like the lemon one so much, actually, because it smells a bit like bathroom cleaner. But around Christmastime she has a cranberry soap that I just love. Anyway, I open her medicine cabinet and there are so many perfumes and lotions and bath salts and magic potions and in the corner on the shelf . . . a bag of razors. The pink ones, with a moisture strip. I saw them in a commercial once. I carefully open the bag while James is playing the piano la-la-la-la-la so no one can hear the crumple sound of the plastic package la-la-la-la and slip one razor into my pocket.

I actually, like, go pee, finally, and come out because it's my turn la-la-la-la-la as though nothing happened.

At home, behind the locked door in the upstairs bathroom, in the tub with the shower curtains drawn, I shave my legs, using soap. After, I wear pants at home to hide my hairless legs from Mom (my legs kind of hurt, like they are burning). I hide the razor, too (under a dresser, wrapped in toilet paper), because if Mom found it, she'd kill me with it.

I wake up early and make boiled eggs and toast. I have hot water and lemon, too, along with a couple of sips of Dad's coffee. I'm ready.

During the verb test, I feel so confident and everything goes smoothly. When I'm done, I walk to the water fountain and let it run for a minute so it doesn't taste like metal and to get it really cold. I gulp so much. I'm so thirsty. When I come up I wipe my mouth with my sleeve and smile and think, *I know I aced it.*

The next day, we get our marks. I got 100 percent. M. Tanguay even drew a happy face at the top of the test.

29

HALLOWEEN! WOOO! Time to have a little fun. I wear a black turtleneck and black jeans and put on one of James's old monster masks from a few years ago. Lame, I know, but it was a last-minute job. I didn't think trick-or-treating was even going to happen this year, because all the parents are afraid of kidnappings and there's some rumor about someone putting razor blades in apples. But then I looked through the window and saw all the small children dressed as ghosts and witches and goblins walking down the street, and Dad said we were allowed to go, but only if he came.

Maybe there's some hope that things might be going back to normal again. I'm so excited and happy that I don't care how lame my thrown-together costume is. Anyway, at this point, it's just about the candy. James wears his skeleton pj's. James, Dad, and I walk across and knock on Nadine's door. I can't wait to see what she's wearing.

But she's just wearing jeans and a guy's oversize white dress shirt (who is she supposed to be, her dad?). Her hair is pulled back in a ballet bun and she's barefoot. "What's going on? Aren't you coming?" I say.

(Nadine: "Hi, Mr. Smith. How are you?")

(Dad: "Good, Nadine. How are you?")

("Well, thank you.")

Nadine to me: "Oh, I forgot to mention . . . I'm not coming."

Me: "Why not?"

"Because Mom said if I stayed home and handed out the candy this year, I could pick the candy. No more mini boxes of raisins," she says, and plops a few lollipops in my pillowcase. "Pure. Hard. Sugar. Can you believe it?"

"Raisins aren't so bad," I say.

"Plus, I want to see all the little kids come to the door and say 'Trick or treat!' They are so cute!"

Jen appears from behind her: peekaboo! She's wearing a pink ball gown and a tiara. I don't think I've ever seen her in a dress before. Maybe at my grandpa's funeral like five years ago, when she wore a black velvet dress with white lace around the collar. Anyway, she's also wearing a sash that says: MISS AMERICA. Her hair is messed up and she painted black circles around her eyes and there is an electrical cord tied around her neck.

Me: "What are you supposed to be?"

Jen: "Electrocuted Miss America."

I laugh because it's pretty genius, you have to admit. But Nadine doesn't and shuts the door quietly. As we turn around and walk down the driveway, I suddenly feel really immature and embarrassed about my costume and about the whole fact that I'm trick-or-treating. I mean, what am I doing? Halloween is for little kids. I have boobs now! I shouldn't be doing this. I should be handing out candy, like Nadine. It's kind of gray and foggy and I sort of want to turn around and go back to Nadine and help her out, but then I glance up at the maple trees in our cul-de-sac and they look like they are on fire, they are glowing so bright. Many of their leaves have fallen down, littering the driveways and sidewalks, and it's so beautiful that I can't stop. From above, I bet it looks as though a pumpkin was dropped and smashed on the city of Surrey, orange pieces everywhere. But really they're fallen leaves.

So I continue and join the unrecognizable neighborhood children in their costumes going up and down the streets and remember how much I love doing this.

Our neighborhood is the best for trick-or-treating. It really is. The best part is that you get to walk through all the streets you don't normally walk down and go into the cul-de-sacs you never go into. You get to see all the houses and how people have decorated them for

Halloween. Some people really go all out and basically make a haunted front yard. But the haunted houses are especially scary this year, considering what happened. One front yard creeps me out a little more than most: piles of dirt to make it look like fresh graves, with an arm poking out of one of them. The arm looks real, too. Like it belongs to a young boy.

As we walk up to one house, I notice that the garage door is halfway open, but I can't see inside because it's dark. This doesn't feel right.

We ring the doorbell and no one answers. I try knocking. Nothing.

Then from over my shoulder, I hear, "Hello."

We scream and turn around, and it's a goblin!

It takes me a second to realize it's a man dressed in a goblin costume (obviously), but it really freaked me out. He goes back into the garage and emerges with a whole chocolate bar each. Not the mini ones. Actual full bars, like the kind you get from the corner store. I'm a little suspicious of this. It's too generous.

Another house gives us a bag of chips, the kind you get in a packed lunch, which happens sometimes, and is less suspicious. I think I'm getting worked up for nothing. Of course, there are a few people who turn off their lights and hide in their houses so they don't have to hand out candy, but it's rare, and we just walk past their houses anyway.

The one strange thing that happens to me as I'm walking around is that I get kinda sad. I think it's because when I'm at home and close my eyes, I can't remember every house in our neighborhood . . . like, exactly. Their shape, their color, what kind of trees and shrubs they have in the yard. It just makes me kind of sad that it's all a blur in my mind. So when I trick-or-treat, I look at everything so hard and try to remember every small detail, but I know I can't because you can't remember everything.

30

AFTER SCHOOL TODAY Mom, out of nowhere, says, "I was married to another man."

She is standing at the kitchen counter cutting long strips from a big chunk of raw beef. For stir-fry, I'm guessing. "To a Korean man," she continues. "Before your dad. Just for a few months." She says this like it's a normal thing to say while handling raw meat. "We came over from Korea for his work. To Calgary. Then stuff happened. Then I met your father."

This is the thing that bothers me about the way Mom talks. It's not her accent or that she doesn't really pronounce things like you should; it's that when she says something, she leaves so many gaps in between bits of information, and it's like she expects me to understand what she hasn't even said.

I'm in my mom's closet, looking through her old photo albums.

In the albums: The pictures are only of her. By a car, on the beach, by a rosebush. I'm trying to find a picture of him. I wonder, if she never broke up with him, would he be my father? Would I even exist? And if I did, would I be full Korean? I wonder if our to-be-born souls are lined up in chronological order or if it depends on who your parents are. I wonder if souls are real at all. I stuff the photo albums in my backpack and go across the street to show them to Nadine and Jen. I hope Nadine is home. *Please be home. Please be home.*

And she is, says Mrs. Ando, who opens the door. I'm hoping this will interest her enough.

The three of us sit on the bottom bunk looking at the photos. Nadine takes the albums and flips through them carefully.

"Look how pretty she is," Nadine says. "Her outfits are so cool. I think those pants might be in style again?"

I can't believe how interested Nadine is. She LOVES these pictures.

"Want to have one to keep?" I say.

"Umm . . . no . . . that's a little . . . They are your mom's. . . ."

"It's no problem," I say.

Jen says, "So what's the deal with these photos?"

"So . . . my mom told me today she was married

before. Can you believe it? I couldn't find any photos with him in it. Do you see him?"

"But he is here," says Jen, who wants to be an investigative reporter. "Just because he isn't in the picture doesn't mean he's not there." She points to one that shows a finger that accidentally slipped across the lens. "He took all these. He was obsessed with your mom. These pictures say that about him. No normal person takes this many pictures of one woman."

Nadine nods. "They are great photos, though."

Then I suddenly remember: In the hallway there's an oil painting on the wall. Of a woman with orange hair. Very abstract. I never noticed it before.

"Who is this supposed to be?" I asked my mom.

Mom: "Me."

"Who painted it?"

"A painter in Korea who was in love with me. He asked me to marry him."

"Really? He proposed?"

"Lots of men did," she says. "You know how pretty I was back then."

"How many proposed?"

"Three. No, four."

"Wow," I say.

"Yeah, well, they were just men. Men who wanted to marry, that's all."

And as I tell this story about my mom and the painting and all the men, Nadine looks down and smiles—even laughs. With her eyes partly closed like that, her eyelashes look like little black fans. I haven't seen Nadine this interested in anything I've had to say in months. Maybe the telling of this story is closing the distance between us. Maybe it reminds her of me and my family and how great we all are together. I hope so.

31

MOM'S OLDEST SISTER, Eemo, is visiting from Korea. She says to me in Korean, "You can start wearing a bit of makeup now. You're old enough."

Every morning, whenever she's here, she and Mom sit on the living room floor with their big metal makeup kits that look like tool kits and examine themselves in their hand mirrors then lightly paint their faces with soft brushes.

One day, Eemo hands me a lipstick. I open it; it's brand-new. It's a shade slightly darker and pinker than my actual lip color. She also gives me a little red compact mirror in the shape of a heart. I put it in my backpack.

The next morning, Mom comes in my room to wake me up. She hands me a pair of short jean shorts from her closet. "They used to be mine," she says. "I think they would look good on you."

I try them on in the bathroom and stand on the bathtub ledge to get a full view in the mirror: They are so short you can almost see my butt cheeks hanging out.

I wear all my new things to school and feel eyes on the top of my thighs.

Even after school, when I'm standing on the side of the road by the school, other kids' moms whisper to each other and look at me from the parking lot. A man with a beard in a blue truck slows down as he drives by. He stops for a second. Then Mom pulls up and I slip in the car and she says, "Very nice! But those are summer shorts! At least wear tights. It's November, crazy girl!" The truck drives off.

That night, I can't sleep again. Why did I do that? How did nobody stop me? Mom didn't notice or care because she was busy with Eemo.

I bet Nadine would have stopped me, because that's what friends do. You need your friends to keep you from wearing embarrassing clothes. I'm so embarrassed that my stomach hurts thinking about it all. I stare up at my glow-in-the-dark stars and close my eyes and the stars are still glowing and dancing in the darkness behind my eyelids and then I open them again.

I wonder if Nadine is in bed too, thinking about me, or of something else, like a math problem or another friend, like Rachel. She must be. She must have someone else to talk to at school. Someone else to do everything with, there.

I can't think about this right now. I can't.

Sleep. Please. Just sleep.

32

YOU KNOW IT'S almost December when your mom packs mandarin oranges in your lunch.

I pull one out and get a whiff. They don't really smell of oranges, but of something else. In the garage, in the Korean fridge, Mom keeps jars of kimchi and hot sauce and baby fish. Sometimes, if there isn't any room in the other fridge, mandarin oranges, too.

I'm standing at the window in class, looking out onto the soccer field and the mountains behind. Snow falls from the sky, like the outside world is a snow globe and someone just shook it, shook us.

"Yay, snowball fights at lunch," says Jen, who is suddenly standing next to me, looking out. "I need to face-wash Josh, to get him back for last year."

She gets serious and says, "Sara, are you okay?"

"What? Why?"

"You seem . . . sad."

I want to tell her everything. About how this has been the worst few months of my life. I look at her and, for the first time, really look at her. And I realize how big and warm her brown eyes are.

"Yah, I'm not doing so well," I say.

"It might be this time of year. Everything gets so quiet," she says. "Also, they haven't found Daniel yet. It'll be harder to search for him with the snow."

I can see our classmates behind us, in the reflection of the window, talking and throwing paper planes because Monsieur Tanguay stepped out to go to the washroom or call his girlfriend or something. And I think, all these kids have no idea what it's like to lose anything.

Monsieur Tanguay comes back with our report cards.

In the hallway, I show my report card to Ms. Lee, holding my thumb on the math mark, which is a B−.

"Congratulations," she says, and pats me lightly on the back.

"All As," I say.

"Great, keep it up."

"I'd like to discuss possibly skipping a grade."

"I didn't realize that was an option for you. Let me talk to Mr. Tanguay."

"I need to know soon."

"I'll get back to you."

It won't be long now until they realize I can skip a grade too, and be closer to my true self.

33

DAD IS DRIVING down Fraser Highway, and on both sides of us is the snow-covered forest. It looks like something out of a fairy tale. There is snow on every single little branch, soft like white fur. When you zoom out and look at it all, as a big picture, it's mainly white everywhere, except for thin black lines, the bits of branches that have decided to reveal themselves ever so slightly. In the distance I see the shape of Mount Baker, but it's white as well. We drive toward it a bit as we head to the mall.

It's not like I believe in Santa or anything, but I'm here to see him. They do a big thing at the mall every year and put up a massive fake Christmas tree decked out in multicolored bulbs and flashing lights, trying to coax people into the Christmas spirit, and it actually kind of works, at least for me.

The best part about Christmas at the mall is that the customer service desk wraps presents for a small donation and they do a pretty good job. Not that I can get many presents with my allowance, but I'll get something for my parents and for James. Anyway, they'll even put ribbon and a bow on the gifts if you want, which is great, especially if you suck at wrapping, like me.

I'm waiting in line with all the little kids and their parents. I wait for a good forty minutes and when it's finally my turn, I march over to Santa and sit on his lap because this needs to be done correctly for it to work.

I whisper in his ear that I want my best friend back, that I want to skip a grade, and that it would be nice if Daniel Monroe was found alive. Santa just stares ahead as the elf girl assistant says, "Smile for the camera." Flash.

Dad is somewhere in the bookstore, where I left him about an hour ago. I told him I needed to get a present for him and that's why I had to be alone. I did get him a mug, by the way, and had it wrapped while I was in line to see Santa, so it's not like I lied that much. Dad was pretty nervous about me walking around the mall alone, but I promised him I wouldn't talk to any strangers.

I look down the various aisles and I can't see him. Then I actually walk down them all, but I still can't find him. I start to panic for a second. Maybe something happened to him. Maybe HE talked to a stranger and is now gone. But then I see the elbow of his brown suede jacket sticking out and he's there, in the corner, sitting on a stepping stool reading a book about a former prime minister, the one he really likes, who always pinned a red rose to his suit.

Dad looks up. "Thank goodness," he says. "You're back."

When we get home, I run upstairs with the photo of the stunned Santa and me on his lap with a blank expression. I put it under my dresser, next to my pink razor blade, as proof that I tried absolutely everything.

34

MOST DAYS DURING the winter break, because the Andos are in Victoria on Vancouver Island and I have nothing to do, I just lie around on the couch under the TV blanket and watch cartoons or old Christmas movies with my brother.

Sometimes . . . I forget about James. I mean, not *forget* forget, but I just, like . . . don't think about him much or . . . ever. I mean, I don't really play with him except when Mom makes us practice our piano duet. And when it just happens.

We used to play a lot more.

I am two years old.

Dad and I go to the hospital and I see Mom. She is lying on the high metal bed holding a blanket and asks me if I want to meet my new little brother, James. Dad picks me up.

He is red and ugly. His face looks like a little bulldog. Ewwwww!!

He's bigger now and looks kind of cute. I drag the yellow laundry basket into the kitchen. I pull James into it with me. And we sit there in the laundry basket for a while, peaceful. It's like our little home.

We make a fort out of sofa cushions, chairs, and bed-sheets. We go inside with a flashlight. Another little home.

We are small.
    We are in the backyard.
    We are in our tae kwon do outfits.
    We stand in front of each other and bow.
    And then we start fighting and we're doing our karate moves and kicks and he punches me in the stomach and he turns and I punch him in the bum and then he comes around and kicks me in the leg and then I start moving my arms like a windmill and go toward him and he starts to run away and then he stops and turns around, starts to do the windmill thing toward me because he's such a copycat and then I run away and then I stop and turn toward him and I do it, I kick him in the privates, and then he falls to the ground and I win, I am the champion!
    Later, in my room, I think, *I'm the worst sister in the world*. But then I get over it. And do it again the next day.

❁

The duck pond down by King George Highway has frozen over and James and I are skating alone together. Usually we come with the Andos, but they are still away. There are tons of other kids around, but we don't know them. The pond freezes to black, not white like the ice rinks. It's a little scary, actually, and for a second when I look down, I think I see a person's face staring up at me through the ice, but I'm just being crazy for a second.

I will say that it is a little iffy for a bunch of people to be skating on a pond. I mean, what if it's thawing? We'd fall through. But people seem convinced it's fine since there are a lot of people skating, though if you think about it, that's when you should avoid the pond because the more people who skate on it, the more likely it'll crack. Anyway, I try to stop thinking about all this.

James and I hold each other's elbows and one of us skates backward as the other skates forward. Then we switch. I'm not sure why we are doing this. Part of it is to practice skating backward, I think, but the other part of it is to see if we can trust the other not to ram us into something. It sounds like a dumb thing to do, but it's pretty fun.

It's Christmas Eve and James and I lie under the Christmas tree, looking up. This is our favorite place. You can't see all the lights twinkling, but you can see the blue and red and yellow glowing in different spots, illuminating certain pine needles, like mini spotlights for those needles. We always put a couple of ornaments under here, near the bottom, just for us to see, like the paper angel and the random red-felt flying boot my aunt made. We want to sleep here, but Mom says it's danger-ous and for us to go to our actual beds.

Later, in bed, I can't fall asleep. I go to James's room and say, "I'm so excited, are you?"

He says, "I'm super excited too. Want to sleep in my room with me?"

"Okay," I say. "But don't pee the bed."

"Okay," he says.

I really hope he doesn't. But I sleep with my arm around him regardless. He's my brother.

35

IT'S CHRISTMAS DAY and we open our presents by the tree and I get a sweater and skirt from "Santa," though, coincidentally, the red ink from the card that says "From Santa" matches the red pen sitting on the kitchen counter. Jeez, Mom and Dad, real smooth.

But James is clueless. He actually still believes. Remember, we're talking about a kid who still pees the bed at the age of ten.

Something slips through the mail slot with a big crash. Which is strange because there is no mail delivery on Christmas Day. On the tile floor is a small rectangular brown box with no Christmas wrapping paper. Written on the side, in black ink: *To Sara. Merry Christmas.*

I rip open the box. It's my favorite perfume! Wait! What?

I look outside through the window, but no one is there.

❁

I lock myself in the bathroom with the perfume. I set it gently on the ledge of the tub and run the bath. As I sink into the hot water, I stare at the bottle through the steam, its shape blurry.

Was it Nadine who gave it to me? But she's away. Maybe she got the mail carrier to do it? But it's Christmas; he isn't working. But she is the only one who knows it is my favorite perfume. I mean, James knows too, but he obviously didn't give it to me because he was sitting next to me opening presents when it came through the slot. Plus, it's in Nadine's nature to give it to me. Like that ice cream cone or that hamster playground. I guess that was technically for Cookie, but still. I can't think of anyone else who would do such a thing.

But then I get scared. Do I have a stalker? Is this someone who is trying to take me, to kidnap me? *Stop being ridiculous,* I think. *It was totally Nadine. She got it to you, somehow. She hasn't forgotten about the things you like.* I calm down and smile. What a sweet surprise. She's the best.

Later, after I step out of my bath and towel myself dry, I squirt the perfume on my wrists, rub them together, then against my neck. I feel so grown and confident and ready for whatever will come next.

36

THE ANDOS ARE home from Vancouver Island, just in time for the annual New Year's Eve party at our place, the best night of the year.

When the doorbell rings, I worry for a slight second that Nadine won't be there. Maybe she's at some cool high school party. But when I open the door and see Mr. and Mrs. Ando, Jen, Megan, *and* Nadine, I am relieved that at least one thing is for sure and will remain the same between our families: our New Year's Eve.

It's about nine o'clock and we perform our annual skit for our parents in our living room. We usually take about half an hour to rehearse right before we perform, and it's always a variation of the same story: A dance teacher is getting the dancers ready for a big competition and the underdog, James, dressed up as a girl, wins. Actually, James doesn't mind dressing up, but I think it may be because he gets to finally win at something in his life, even though he has to pretend to be a ballerina, and a girl, to do so. I was going to direct this year, but Nadine came up with the variation on the story and of course she's always the lead actor and dancer, obviously, because she is so good. I can tell she's really into it. It's our best play yet. And for most of the night, it feels like the good old times.

Except for certain things. Nadine and I don't sit next to each other at the kids' dinner table in the family room. I wind up between James and Jen. We also don't run up to my room to get away from everyone and play on our own for a bit. I'm kind of looking for a moment to tell her that I might be skipping a grade as well. Or at least that the vice principal is considering it.

But we all just sit downstairs most of the time, on the couch, watching the pre-show before the dropping of the ball in Times Square in New York City.

Nadine casually says, "I wasn't even going to come tonight."

"Oh?"

"Yes, I was supposed to babysit Mom's friend's baby while she and her husband went out. But they canceled because the baby is sick and so they decided to stay home. I'm pretty sad. It would have been my first baby-sitting job."

"Well, it's a good thing they canceled. We got to do the play. It's tradition."

"I guess," she says. "But I really could have used the money. I want to buy some new clothes."

"Yeah," I say. The crack in my voice startles me as I realize that Nadine thinks new clothes are more important than me. I try to change the subject. "Or you could have bought more perfume."

"Perfume? I guess so."

I knew it! She did get it for me but is being oddly secretive about it still. Maybe she doesn't want her parents or Jen to overhear that she spent so much money on me.

It's midnight and we make noise with paper trumpets and these winding rattle things. Mrs. Ando gives us sparklers and lights them for us. Nadine, Jen, and I go outside and they look like mini fireworks against the black-and-navy-marbled sky. We all dance around together yelling, "Happy New Year!" up at the sky. This coming new year will be better than the last—I can feel it. It's only up from here.

When the sparklers go out, Nadine quickly runs back inside, mumbling that it's cold, thinking that we are following. But Jen and I stay outside together for a while longer, for some reason, and keep cheering and being loud.

Suddenly, a big light in the sky circles around and then goes behind the forest, or in it, I'm not sure, and we run inside and slam the door and Jen says, "Sara, I think we just saw a UFO."

37

NEW YEAR'S DAY. Mom dresses me in a hanbok. It's pink, and a white ribbon ties me up at the chest like I'm a present. James just wears a suit.

Our whole family drives to Auntie Moon's house in Burnaby. When we get there, Auntie Moon and Uncle Dong put their arms around us and scoop us in. They leave the front door slightly open. "It's so the spirits of our ancestors can come in," Auntie Moon says.

On a low Korean table: There are pictures of their ancestors in black and white. They are the same ones Auntie Moon puts on display every year and they always freak me out because no one is smiling. It's like they looked dead already when the photos were taken. It's so weird.

Uncle Dong's mom sits in an armchair. She's super old and every year I wonder if the next time there will be a picture of her, too, on that table. That sounds so bad, but it's true. I'm not trying to be mean. People die, and it's so sad.

We all sit around the kitchen table and eat some ddukguk, the lucky New Year's soup with meat, garlic, green onion, and rice cakes cut into little discs. I have mine topped with roasted seaweed and egg. Mom says by eating it we become a year older. I eat three bowls to make sure this happens. And then Uncle Dong says, "It's time."

Uncle Dong and Auntie Moon sit on the couch in the living room. And James and I stand before them. We do a full bow, our bodies folding over toward the floor.

And then they hand us each a white envelope with money in it. And then we have to listen to their lesson: "Study hard at school and practice piano well."

Then James and I stand before Uncle Dong's mom and bow and listen to another lesson. She speaks in Korean, and Mom translates: "Listen to your parents," she says. "Especially you, Sara. Listen to your mom."

But I swear she didn't say this, because I understand Korean and my mom seems to forget this fact whenever it's convenient. She just added that last part. She's such a scammer.

Later that night, I'm watching TV alone. I flip through the channels.

I watch a man in a beige trench coat and a kind of scary voice walking down the street and talking about the biggest unsolved mysteries in America. Ghosts, sea monsters, alien abductions. I wonder if they are going to mention the UFO in Surrey last night. But then I realize this is a rerun.

Flip.

Another man talking about the biggest kidnapping cases in America. I wonder if they'll ever talk about the one that happened here, in Canada. I wonder if they'll ever find Daniel.

38

FIRST DAY BACK at school and I can't even write the right year on the top of my assignments. This happens at the beginning of every new year, for like a month. It's kind of annoying and dumb.

But what's even more annoying is that I keep calling Nadine and she's never home. I want to tell her that I might be skipping and I need tips and pointers about everything. I want to know how it all went down for her. Did she have a meeting with the teacher and principal? Every time I call, Mrs. Ando says she's busy or not home and that she'll get her to call me back. What the heck.

One night, I call a couple of times, then Mrs. Ando calls back and asks for my mom. I pass the phone over. I hear Mom say, "Yes, I understand. Thanks, Kelly," and then she comes to me and says I need to stop calling the Andos so much. That it's disruptive or something.

Oh.

And I wonder . . . did Nadine tell her mom to say

that? Is she home and avoiding me? Why doesn't she want to speak to me? It's only a phone call; it's not like I'm going over there and bugging her all night. I just want to see what is up and tell her a few things. Or maybe Mrs. Ando is seriously super annoyed with me? Does she not want me to play with her daughter? Am I that bad? I want to call and find out, and I lift the receiver but put it down again, because that'll just make things worse.

Before lunch the next day, an announcement: "Sara Smith, there is a message for you at the office."

At first I think that maybe Mom surprised me with a burger and fries as a treat. Yes! Wait, but then my brother would have been called too, because she wouldn't just get it for me.

I go down to the office and Ms. Lee is standing there and waving for me to follow her inside. M. Tanguay rushes in.

"Oh, Monsieur," I say.

"Bonjour," M. Tanguay says.

"Sara. Thanks for coming. We have some news for you," Ms. Lee says.

"Oh . . . you do?" Then I realize that both the vice principal and my teacher have called a meeting with me. This can only mean one thing. It's actually happening!

M. Tanguay starts. He's speaking in English, which is

weird, but I guess it's for Ms. Lee. "You're doing very well in school, Sara. Nearly straight As. Except math. You have a B−. However, you've shown great improvements lately. I think you could get an A if you really wanted to."

"Oh, of course I could get an A, no problem."

Ms. Lee continues, "Unfortunately, we don't recommend putting you ahead a year. We don't think it's the best choice for you. To skip a grade, you not only have to display certain outstanding academic capabilities, but it requires a certain set of social and emotional capabilities to be in class with people who are older."

"You think I'm immature?"

"No!" M. Tanguay says. "You're perfect for your age. You're doing well in grade seven. We just think that putting you a year ahead will not be good for you. Sometimes, it's better for some people to be at the top of the class."

Ms. Lee says, "We know your friend Nadine skipped a grade. I'm sure that's why you want to skip, but what's right for her isn't necessarily right for you. We think you are where you need to be, and it's a great place to be."

"You are a leader in the class," M. Tanguay says. "Tes camarades de classe ont besoin de toi."

Back in class, I pretend like that whole conversation didn't happen, but M. Tanguay keeps looking at me in a concerned way. I tell him I'm not feeling well and need to go to the nurse's office. I point to my stomach to hint that it's pain from my period, even though I don't have my period yet. This makes him feel awkward, yet compassionate, and he lets me go.

I lie on the high examination table/bed with the tissue running down the middle. It makes an annoying crinkly sound every time I move so I try to stay as still as possible.

That's it, I give up. It's over. I won't be going to high school to be with Nadine this year. I'll just stay here and be alone. I look around the room. The walls are bare and the room smells like cleaner. A single fluorescent light beam flickers. Suddenly I feel as empty as this room. I don't feel like crying, which is weird. I just feel nothing. Tired.

Since there is no nurse here, except for when we get immunizations, the secretary checks in on me. I ask her to call home to get my mom to pick me up because even though I'm stuck here, in elementary school, where the most thrilling thing that can happen to you is finding string cheese in your lunch, I can't bear to be here right now. I just want to be home with my family.

39

U.S., CANADA, U.S., Canada, U.S., Canada. James and I jump back and forth from one country to the other. We always do this when we're at the border. It can be pretty fun to play with my brother.

Mom and Dad are in the van, in the lineup that stretches so long and moves so slowly there is almost always enough time to get out and play. We're in the green park in the middle of all the cars where there is this big white arch that celebrates the point where Canada and the U.S. meet.

Underneath the arch is where the real border is. I put my left leg in Canada, my right one in the U.S. "Hey, I'm half Canadian, half American," I say. James copies me. He always does.

The U.S. customs officer asks: "Citizenship?"

Dad: "Canadian."

"All of you?"

"Yes."

The officer, to Mom: "And you? What are you?"

"Canadian," she says.

"And these are your kids?"

"Yes," she says.

He looks at us for a long time. Finally he says, "Go ahead."

We drive ahead.

"Wow," Dad says. "Can you believe him?"

Mom says nothing, pretending like what just happened didn't happen. But I'm so mad. I mean, really? Who does he think he is? We look just like Mom, especially James. I hate it when people think we are not hers. I hate it when they treat her like this and think we don't notice because we are kids. I hate people, sometimes.

Anyway.

We're going to Seattle for the night. The border is only a twenty-minute drive from our house, and Seattle's about a two-hour drive from there depending on traffic. We're going to visit Samchoon, Mom's older brother, my uncle. We go to Seattle several times a year to see him.

"He's like my father," Mom says, sitting in the front seat. I-5 stretches ahead of us. "Since my dad died when I was ten, he gave me away at our wedding."

Samchoon lives in this small two-bedroom apartment. James and I have to sleep in the living room when we stay, but it has the most beautiful view of the harbor so I don't mind. Seattle looks quite a lot like Vancouver. Except for the small differences, which I can't describe, as they are there but so small and I'm still trying to figure them out.

Dad takes James and me to Pike Place Market. We eat mussels for the first time in a restaurant. Little rubber balls that taste like butter and garlic.

We watch men in the market shout and yell and Dad says, "Go tell them you want to buy a fish," and when I do they toss the fish back and forth from one guy to another and a little crowd gathers as they do this until it's in a little package ready for us to take home.

As we walk through the market, past all the buckets of flowers, I see a flash of blond and blue ahead of me and I weave through the crowd to see if it's Daniel until he disappears by blending into the fruit stand and Dad grabs my shoulder and says, "We almost lost you."

That night, I finally get my period. It isn't the biggest deal; I knew it was coming someday soon because I have boobs now. And at school they've been making us watch videos on puberty since, like, grade four, so I knew what to expect. Mom gives me one of her maxi pads. Great, now Cookie and I both use them. Anyway, my stomach hurts quite a lot so all I eat is cereal.

But I wish I could tell Nadine. I know she hasn't gotten hers . . . unless she has and hasn't told me. I want to tell her how it felt like I peed a little bit by accident in my underwear because it was wet, but it wasn't pee, it was my period. And that it was more pink than red. I also want to tell her about the cramps. They really suck.

Maybe I'll tell Nadine right when I get back. I will tell Jen, for sure, too. If only to explain the reason behind the frequent trips I'll almost definitely have to make to the washroom when at school. I'm also going to have to ask her to keep an eye on my butt in case I leak through my clothes. I'm a little bit worried about that.

We're all asleep on the way home. Except Dad, who's driving, thank God. For some reason, I always wake up the exact moment we're about to enter the cul-de-sac, like my body somehow knows when I'm about to come home.

I look across the street. I see a blond girl standing at the Andos' door. A blond girl with natural highlights. The door opens. And she goes inside.

That's it, I think. I won't tell Nadine about my period. Maybe I won't tell her anything ever again.

40

I LOOK IN the cage: Cookie is gone.

I call the Andos. Both Nadine and Jen come over. I don't care about what has happened. This is an emergency. It's life or death. I can't think straight. I'm full-on panicking.

We are upstairs in my room, staring at his cage. I need them to tell me where to start looking. Jen crouches down to inspect the cage and points to the wire door.

"It seems as though Cookie was able to open the door a bit somehow and slip through a teeny-weeny gap," she says. We look through my room, carefully picking up each piece of clothing on the floor, in case he crawled into a sleeve or a pocket to have a nap.

"Oh no," I say.

"What?" asks Nadine.

"I just realized . . . he's not necessarily still upstairs."

"What do you mean?"

Jen: "Yeah, how can a hamster know how to go down-stairs?"

Me: "Because I trained him to."

Them, together: "What?"

"It was last year. Remember when I was really freaked out about house fires?"

Nadine: "Oh yeah. You made us figure out an escape plan from our bedroom. You got Dad to climb down a pipe."

Me: "Yeah, well, so anyway, I trained Cookie how to go downstairs. Just in case. So he could get out safely."

Jen: "Oh my God. We are so screwed."

Nadine starts to pace around the room and then sits on my bed for a good few minutes. After a while she says, "Where is the hamster food?"

Me: "In the laundry room."

The three of us go downstairs. We stand on the cold floor, not quite sure what to do next. Then I just blurt out, "Cookie, come here!"

And from behind the dryer, we hear a little noise. Then we see a little nose poke out from behind the dryer. A little nose with some black dust on its tip.

It's Cookie, and he comes running straight to me. I scoop him up and give him a hug, a special kind of hug you can only give a cute little hamster. And I'm so completely relieved and happy to have found my best little buddy.

✾

A few weeks later, Cookie makes the ultimate escape. He dies. At the age of four years, four months, and four days.

We hold a funeral in our backyard. Under the big cedar tree. All its needles are a deep green though it's still technically winter. The trees in Canada don't die.

Jen is the priest. Everyone has come: Nadine, Megan, and my brother. We make a half circle around the trunk of the tree. We're all wearing black. And I wear Mom's black sunglasses.

Jen has dug a little grave and has nailed two twigs together in a cross and stuck it into the ground. She starts reciting stuff that sounds like it could be from the Bible, but it's not, she's just making it up. I'm holding the brown paper bag with Cookie inside. I slip one half of the BFF golden pendant heart that I was going to give Nadine into the bag because it should be with Cookie, he was my true best friend who never betrayed me. Jen takes the paper bag and places it in the little hole. I throw bright yellow dandelions on top.

Jen puts her arm around me and says, "He lived a long life." And I look from the grave up the tree, along the long trunk, all the way up. And I wonder if there is a kind of God out there and if there is, if he can tell me if my hamster is in heaven or hell, or whether he will be reincarnated as a cat or a dog or a blade of grass.

"Heaven," Jen says. "Obviously. Hamsters go straight

to heaven." But I hope he reincarnates into something, like a dog, so I can see him again. I'm not sure anymore about anything, though, and then Jen hugs me. Big and warm. And Nadine just stands there.

The next day the doorbell rings, and there is an envelope, and in it, a small card with a drawing of a hamster with a halo on it. "I'm sorry about Cookie," it reads. I think it's Nadine finally telling me how sorry she is.

41

FRIDAY NIGHT phone call to the Andos. I haven't called in a while so I think it's okay.

"Hello?" (It's Mrs. Ando.)

"Hi, it's Sara." *Please don't be mad. Please don't be mad,* I think.

"Hi, dear." Phew.

"Sorry to bother you, but is Nadine around? I wondered if she wants to sleep over tonight. It's been a while and I thought it might be fun."

"Oh, she didn't tell you?"

"No. What?"

"She's actually over at her friend Rachel's house tonight. They are working on a project."

"Does Rachel have natural highlights?"

"Are those natural?"

I can't breathe. Then I say, I don't know why, "Is Jen home?"

"Oh, sure. Hold on. Jen! Phone!"

Me: "Hey, it's me."

Jen: "Hey, what's up?"

"Not much. Want to sleep over tonight?"

"Really?"

"Yeah."

"Totally! I'll come right over."

"Perfect."

42

THE LIGHT IS blinding. And just when it's about to get to be too much, Dr. Chiang's head hovers above me to block it. With huge pliers, he begins pulling each square of metal off my teeth. There is a CRACK every time he does this, and I worry that he's taking my teeth off too.

I think about trying to get up and out, but like an alien who has ESP, his assistant holds me down and says, "Just hang on, we're not done yet." Then Dr. Chiang pulls out a little drill that makes the most annoying high-pitched sound I've ever heard. I swear, if you listened to it long enough, your brain would explode. He drills away at my teeth, little bits of old glue spewing out of my mouth, like cement. And the smell. Oh, the smell. I don't think I'll ever forget that strange burnt smell, like how I'll never forget the smell when they re-tarred the school's roof.

"All done," he says at last. I walk over to the washroom and rinse my mouth and splash water on my face.

As I'm doing this, I look in the mirror, and it's almost as though I don't recognize myself anymore. Like the braces coming off actually changed the shape of my face or something to make it look a bit sharper or older, maybe a bit skinnier. And then I run my tongue over my teeth and around my mouth, and I feel kinda naked. This feels really different.

43

I THINK MY boobs have grown again. Because in the girls' changing room, getting ready for gym class, Jen randomly blurts out: "Sara, you should wear a bra."

"What?"

"YOU SHOULD WEAR A BRA. YOUR BOOBS ARE HUGE."

"I wear a training bra," I say. Some of the girls are watching us, looking at me. How embarrassing.

"NEWS FLASH: It's not working. You need the industrial-strength kind. Those are bouncing around and stuff. Especially in gym class. It gets Ricky Grant all excited."

During gym class:

We are playing dodgeball. I run and jump and dive to avoid being hit by the balls.

I look at Ricky.

And then I look down.

Eww.

Mom is driving me and Jen to Guildford Mall to buy me a bra. I always thought I'd be with Nadine when I bought my first real, adult bra, but here I am with Jen. I'm okay with it, actually, because I don't get really embarrassed around her and don't worry about things like how I look or how my body is changing. I do a bit more when I'm with Nadine.

Suddenly Mom says to us, "You must make sure you have lots of experience with guys before you get married."

"Uh, okay," I say. "What do you mean?"

"You know, sex."

"Mom! I'm twelve!"

Jen laughs so hard so quietly, her laugh goes back into her lungs and she chokes.

"I know. I mean, I'd kill you if you even kiss a guy now. But just so you know. For later on."

We are at a stoplight. Mom turns and looks at us in the back.

"All these guys now, you can't see them as permanent people," she says. "The first guy you meet won't be the last guy. Remember that."

"Did you have lots of experience with guys?" I ask.

"Are you kidding?" she says, looking back at the road. "I married your dad when I was thirty-three; what do you think? And I was really pretty. Still am." She drives ahead. Sometimes it surprises me that Mom doesn't seem to care what people think of her. She's confident like that. Sometimes I wish I were more like her.

It's so funny watching Mom park in a parking lot. I always wondered what criteria she has for choosing a parking spot. I used to think she would only park in spots where there were no oil stains on the cement, and then I thought she parked only next to nice cars, and then I thought she parked where there were no cars around, but now I've come to the conclusion that she just randomly parks wherever.

I'm over at the Andos'. But I'm here because Jen invited me, not Nadine. Being in the house feels different because of this. The house also looks different, and I see details I've never noticed before. Like the shelf in the laundry room where they put the different kinds of soap in a line. The corner in the living room where Mrs. Ando has her desk. The silver goose paperweight on top of a stack of bills.

Nadine is upstairs, in her room, with the door closed. Doing homework, I think. She hasn't really come down to say hi. Jen and I are in the family room, watching a taped episode of *Unsolved Mysteries*. Jen says we have to watch it considering what we saw on New Year's Eve.

This episode is about four guys who go camping, and while canoeing late one evening, they see a light in the sky following them. After canoeing for about twenty minutes, they return to their camp, but the fire they built to last all night is already out, confirming they were away a lot longer than they thought. Once they're back home, they all start separately experiencing nightmares about being abducted by aliens.

Nadine is suddenly downstairs, in the kitchen, making a cup of tea. Since when does she drink tea? She told me once that it tastes like dishwater. I pretend not to see her as she comes over quietly to see what we are watching. I already know that she won't be interested in the show. Nadine is a girl of science and reason. Jen is too, but I feel like Jen is more open to the unknown, like me. Nadine leans against the wall and watches the show for about one minute, just long enough for it to register that it is not her thing, then she leaves and goes back upstairs, without knowing that all the while, I was watching her from the corner of my eye.

It feels a little wrong to be here at the Andos' house like this.

44

JEN IS SLEEPING OVER. We're in my bed. It's late. Almost midnight. The stars are out, both outside the window and above our heads, stickers glowing on the ceiling. There is one little moon sticker that looks like a ripped-off fingernail.

We're waiting for it to be exactly midnight to go downstairs and have a snack. Because you can't call it a midnight snack otherwise, you know. We are talking about ghosts.

Jen says, "I totally believe in ghosts."

"Me too," I say.

A sparkle in Jen's eye. She says, "Hey, let's make a pact. That when we die we are going to come back and haunt your house."

"Cool," I say.

We get out of bed and grab a piece of paper from my desk and write, *TO WHOEVER SHOULD FIND THIS: SARA AND JEN WILL COME BACK AND HAUNT YOU!!*

We roll the paper up in a tube, tiptoe downstairs, and put it in the crawl space in the closet.

We go back upstairs.

I unfold the Ouija board and place it on my bedroom floor. Jen and I put our fingers lightly on the kind-of-heart-shaped piece of plastic.

Somehow I convinced Mom to buy me a Ouija board, promising her I'd get an A in math and practice piano lots, which she fell for, and which I actually kind of believed too. I think she thought it was just like any other board game, like Monopoly. They didn't have Ouija boards in Korea, I'm guessing.

"Is somebody here?" I ask.

The kind-of-heart plastic thing moves quickly across the board to YES.

Jen: "Are you alive or dead?"

Ouija board: "D . . . E . . . A . . . D."

Us: "Ahhhhhhhhhhh!!"

Jen: "This is freaky, let's stop."

Me: "No, no, no."

"My mom said these things are evil," she says.

"I thought you are an atheist," I say.

"I am, but my mom is Catholic."

Me, heart pounding: "I have a question. Is Daniel Monroe dead or alive?"

"A . . . L . . . I . . . V . . . E."

Jen: "Oh my God."

Me: "Where is he?"

"S . . . A . . ."

"Where is that?"

"S.A.T."

"Saturday?"

"NO."

"What, then?"

"S.A.T.A.N."

Jen and I scream and I fold up the board and we bury it in my closet and never open it again.

"We were talking to the devil," I say. "This thing is evil!"

"Satan's not real," Jen says. "I think."

A few days later:

On the welcome mat at the front door I find a small box of chocolates. I open it and the chocolates are in the shape of hedgehogs, my favorites. Okay . . . only one person knows I love that kind of chocolate. One person. There is also a note put together with cut-out letters from a magazine to spell "You're sweet." I look around and see nothing and sprint across the street and knock on the door and no one answers so I yell: "Nadine! Nadine, please come out! I know it was you who gave me the chocolates! Thank you!"

A guy is walking his Chihuahua by the cul-de-sac and I feel him noticing me and thinking I'm crazy so I start running like I'm just casually exercising and start singing really loud so he thinks I was just practicing for choir or something and I turn around and run home, thinking, how did she get them to me and why is she keeping it a secret?

45

A DREAM: A boy, who looks like Daniel Monroe but isn't him because he looks older and has darker hair and isn't quite like how the computer-generated photos made him out to be, opens the door. A waft of air from his house hits me in the face. I smell laundry detergent and strawberries.

"Hi," I say.

He says nothing and takes my hand. Leads me up the stairs, into his blue bedroom. He keeps the light off. He lets go of my hand and sits on his unmade bed as I stay standing in the doorway. We stare at each other in silence. He pats the bed next to him and says, "Come here." I do.

Sitting side by side on his bed, we are facing his shelf full of hockey trophies and medals. "Wow," I say. "You win a lot."

He puts his left hand on my right knee and then glides it upward until it's at the middle of my thigh. I look down to make sure he doesn't go any higher and he turns toward me and with his right hand he lightly cups my cheek and pulls my face toward him until he's slurping in my mouth, his tongue fat and wide, almost choking me. But we settle into a rhythm and I'm okay and we make out for a while.

I wake up and go downstairs. Mom is out. Dad is watching a documentary on WWII. "Hello," he says. He looks at me awkwardly, then jumps up and goes upstairs. And watches TV from there. He knows.

The next day:

Ricky Grant corners me in the hall to tickle me; I don't know why. He tickles me on the hips and then he grazes my right boob with his knuckles and it surprises me and I try to push him away. And he comes up again and pushes me against the wall and presses himself up against me and then Ms. Lee walks around the corner and Ricky walks away and I feel so disgusted with myself. I'm so gross.

46

AT BEAR CREEK PARK. Running around the track, which is burnt orange and circles around a green football field. I run on the inside track.

In my line of vision: The green of the field up against the orange of the track. It's so beautiful.

And the colors match the saris of the Indian women walking around and around slowly in their white running shoes while their husbands sit at the picnic tables. They sit there with these tall turbans on, with these long gray beards trickling down. And they look as though they are debating the inner mysteries of the world.

They watch me as I run around, like they know everything about me and everything I've thought and done that was wrong or dishonest or selfish. They can see me for who I really am.

47

IT'S VALENTINE'S DAY. Before class, by the coatrack, as we are all putting our backpacks and jackets on our hooks, Josh gives me and Jen one yellow rose each. It's wrapped in clear cellophane with gold stars on it and it crinkles under my fingertips when I hold it.

"Yellow represents friendship," he says.

For the rest of the day, I notice the color of gold everywhere. The gold in some dead grass, the gold of Dad's wedding ring, the gold in Jen's skin.

I'm at the Andos' waiting for Jen to come downstairs. We're going to a movie.

Nadine is sitting at the kitchen table with her friend Rachel; they're sipping on bowls of miso soup. It's the first time I've seen Rachel this close. She is really beautiful. Nadine was right.

"Hey," Rachel says.

"Oh," Nadine says. "This is Sara. She lives across the street."

"Hi."

Rachel: "Oh, are you going to hang with us?"

Nadine: "Actually, she's here for my sister."

"Oh, right," Rachel says. "Cool."

Nadine, jokingly: "Yeah, actually she used to be my best friend but then dumped me for my sister." She laughs, though there is a crack in her voice.

Hold on. She thinks I'm the one who . . . wait . . . What is going on? I'm suddenly really confused and I open my mouth to speak, but nothing comes out. I want to say that I'm here and that I've always been here. *I didn't mean to hurt you, Nadine. Or for it to seem like I left you for someone else.*

Jen comes in and says, "Let's go. I'm starving. I am going to eat so much popcorn."

As we walk along their driveway to meet my dad, who is driving us to the theater, I see Nadine's silhouette through the window. She is near the sink with both her arms on the counter kind of propping her up. Her head is down.

After the movie, when I get home, there's one red rose on the doorstep and I pick it up and look back at the Ando house and I know she gave it to me.

48

IT'S SUNDAY MORNING and I'm over at the Andos'. Jen and I are in the living room, asleep in our sleeping bags in front of the television. We forgot to turn it off last night so some cartoons are now on because it's the morning.

I feel someone in the room. I open my eyes: Nadine.

She tiptoes over us, light on her ballet feet, and grabs the remote to turn the TV off. She then hops over both of us, landing perfectly on her tippy-toes again. She quietly goes into the kitchen.

I get up and follow her.

"Hi," I say.

"Oh. Did I wake you? I'm sorry."

"No. I was already awake."

She is standing at the counter with a box of cinnamon buns from the mall and a knife.

"Want one?" she asks.

"Sure."

She pulls one out of the box and gooey strings are

attached to it, it's that sticky, and puts it on a pink plate. The next one goes on a purple plate. Our old favorite colors. I guess maybe they still are our favorite colors. I don't know anymore. "Thanks," I say.

Silence.

And then she says, "So how are you?"

"Pretty good," I say. "How are you?"

"I'm fine," she says. She pulls out the soft center of her cinnamon bun and puts it in her mouth. That's her favorite part. I like the outside part better.

I ask, "What are you doing up so early?"

"I don't know. I like mornings."

"Me too."

Silence, again.

Nadine: "I'm really sorry that I was such a cow about the search for that boy way back. They still haven't found him. Even though I didn't know him, I miss him."

I start to cry a little.

And then I say: "Nadine, what happened to us?"

And right at that moment Jen comes in and says, "Woo-hoo! Cinnamon buns!"

And Nadine looks at me, as though saying, "I'm not sure."

The other day at the grocery store:

We are all at the checkout counter, waiting for Mrs. Ando to pay. Nadine is there. She's standing by her mom, with a brand-new white leather purse over her shoulder.

She sees a little donation box on the counter for the Children's Hospital. She opens her purse and takes out her wallet and pours all her change into it.

That's the thing about Nadine. She's got a good heart. And I realize that lately I've only been seeing the moments when she seems mean or cold, but she's not. She is generous and selfless. She never talks about herself much, like I do, and she always asks people questions about themselves and generates conversation, which I'm not really good at. She always listened to me, you know. And she never really gets jealous or says anything nasty about anyone and never seeks attention. I can't say the same about myself.

49

SPRINGTIME FLOATS ABOVE me and opens up
and pulls me out of winter. Things are looking brighter
again. Literally. Like everything in my vision is a few
shades lighter than it was before.

I'm at Josh's bar mitzvah party. Everyone in class got
invited. It's at the fanciest hotel in Surrey, the one next
to the highway.

Anyway, I've been waiting for this party since forever.
Well, since Josh told me about it in grade five. He sat in
front of me all year and then one day he turned around
and said, "When I turn thirteen, I'm going to have the
BEST party ever and you're invited."

In the hotel:

We swim around in the biggest pool. I look up, way
up, through the glass window up to the sky. Waiters
in white tuxedos come out and serve us orange juice
in champagne glasses and we sit around in the hot tub
sippin' it like movie stars.

Josh's parents rented two rooms for us to get ready in after the swim. One for the girls, one for the boys. All the girls go into our room, giggling; we can't believe how cool this is. We all change, making sure to cover ourselves with our towels and putting our bras and underwear on under them.

I'm staring at myself in the mirror. I pull my hair up, twist it, and tuck it into itself with a million pins to keep it from swooping down. Then I slip on a black dress. My mom made it. Pull on long black gloves up my right arm, up my left arm, little white pearls embroidered around their edges. They're my mom's. Then pearls around my neck and some pinned in my ears. I'm trying to look like a silent film movie star. At least, that is my goal. I probably look on the edge of just weird. But that's okay.

In the ballroom downstairs:

I eat salmon for dinner and drink ice water out of a wineglass and have the fluffiest chocolate cake for dessert and then everyone gets up. All of Josh's family forms a circle and holds hands and we go around and around and around and it's so much fun, and then Jen grabs me because she is so crazy and says she feels like a Slurpee, so we leave and run across the street to the gas station with the *tap tap tap* of our dress shoes and the twinkle twinkle twinkle of the streetlights, and we buy cherry Slurpees not caring that one of the parents will find out that we were out at night alone because we quickly go back to the hotel and nobody knows that we've been gone because we've downed our Slurpees so fast and have brain freeze, but then we dance some more and it's better. We do this until midnight.

My dad picks me and Jen up.

In the back of the minivan:

We have our feet up, they hurt so much. And I think, *This was the best night of my life.*

50

IT'S SCARLETT DAVIES'S birthday. I'm kind of surprised she invited me. We're not really friends, but I think she invited most of the grade seven girls. Jen wasn't invited. Or Nadine. People have already forgotten about her being at our school, it seems.

We're at the Stardust roller rink. Scarlett's mom sits in the corner, with a melting ice cream cake on the table, and smokes.

We buy glow-in-the-dark sticks on shoestrings and put them around our necks. There is a disco ball. It makes speckles of light dance all over the place.

On the roller rink:

We all skate around in a circle, me, Scarlett, Heather, but they are really slow so I go ahead a bit. Some guy is skating backward and a few people skate holding hands, but no, not me—I'm skating ALONE! As fast as I can! And I cross my legs one over the other and let my hair flap against the wind and I feel so free and I can't believe it, I'm not thinking of anything, not of Nadine, or Daniel going missing, I'm just skating faster and faster and I pass everyone over and over and I feel FREE from EVERY-ONE and EVERYTHING and this LIFE!

Scarlett catches up with me and suddenly it's the two of us together. "You're an awesome skater! Super fast."

Afterward, we pull off our skates and go outside and I'm so shocked by the light, kind of like when you come out of the theater after an afternoon show, it seems as though it should be dark, but it's not. "Strange, isn't it?" Scarlett says as though she read my thoughts. Then I realize I forgot to tell Dad when to pick me up. "Need a ride home? We go right by your house anyway," she says.

51

I'M SUPPOSED TO be working on a project for the science fair with Jen. It's about the effects of oil spills on the environment and wildlife and the best ways to contain the damage. And though the images of birds covered in grease not being able to breathe are super sad and made me want to work on the project to make a difference, I decide to go downtown on the SkyTrain with Scarlett to go shopping.

I tell Mom that we are going with her mom, but we're not. We're going alone. I'm a little scared.

We get on the train and sit next to each other on the red and blue plastic seats and ride all the way into downtown, get out at Granville Street station, and go up the escalators that are so steep you feel like you are going to fall down.

We walk along Robson Street, past the art gallery, and through a coffee shop window I see Ms. Lee with a woman. Ms. Lee is smiling and looking down and turning her coffee cup counterclockwise. Some boys sitting outside up against the shop window look at us and one says, "Nice legs! Yum-yum!" Ms. Lee looks up, surprised to see us in the window, and I grab Scarlett and we run away, get on the train, and go straight home, totally freaked. We don't really talk about how it wasn't quite as fun as we thought it would be to go downtown alone, and though I don't tell her, I never want to do it again.

That day, they find Daniel Monroe's dad's body somewhere in a shallow grave near Lake Ontario. The news says that the body decomposed for a while, possibly over a year. "It means he didn't take him," James says. "I knew it! I knew it!"

"But it means that someone murdered his dad at some point," I said. James is suddenly quiet.

The phone rings. I already know who it is.

"So I guess it's official," Jen says. "Some stranger took him."

"Yes, I guess so."

"We have to be more careful," she says. "It was dumb of us to run to the gas station in the middle of the night to get those Slurpees."

"Yes, let's not do anything like that again," I say, thinking of my downtown trip with Scarlett that Jen doesn't know about.

"Anyway, we have to work on our science project soon," she says.

"The fair isn't till next week," I say. "We have tons of time. Relax."

"We don't have tons of time."

"Well, I don't have time to work on it right now. I'm really busy."

"Sure. Me too. Excuse me, I have to shave my legs and put makeup on."

She hangs up on me. I think she was being sarcastic. Can you believe it?

In class, guys are passing around notes saying, "Do you like me?" with a checkbox next to the word "Yes" and another next to the box "No." When I get one, I add an extra box to make "Maybe" and I check that off just to mess with them.

Anyway, Scarlett and I are elected as copresidents of the grade seven prom committee. We decided that no grade sixers are allowed at the prom. "It's because they get one next year anyway," we explain to the class, just before recess.

I look at Jen to see how she reacts. She just sits there with her arms crossed. What's with her attitude these days?

52

SO I DIDN'T get a good mark on my science quiz today but it doesn't matter because I'm not skipping anyway and it's just not how my brain works so whatever. I do have the science fair coming up, so I can bring up my grade if I work hard on the project, but why should I bother? I need to respect my natural tendencies and not do things that I don't enjoy because life is short.

Life is not all about studying and skipping grades. It's about feeling good and having fun and hanging out with fun girls like Scarlett and people my own age and grade who have the same interests and appreciate me for who I am. Should I tell Mom about my science grade? Maybe not . . .

53

I'M PRACTICING PIANO. I have this competition coming up soon so I figure I have to put some time in.

Outside, Jen is playing hockey with Josh and the Singh boys. It's the first time I've seen them playing since last summer because the Singh boys weren't allowed to play outside all year. I press hard on the keys, loud, to see if she can hear me, but she doesn't, or at least pretends she doesn't, she just laughs and takes slap shots at the net. Then, all of a sudden, I see Nadine run out of her house holding a pair of jeans and yelling at her sister.

I continue to play.

As Nadine approaches, Jen shakes her head no and laughs, and Nadine suddenly grabs Jen's arm and forces her to look again.

Oh no.

Jen spins and elbows Nadine in the stomach by accident. Nadine releases Jen's arm and holds her stomach and charges for Jen, who ducks away, and Nadine almost falls. They are just standing there yelling in each other's faces. There is nothing I can do because I'm not done practicing piano and my mom would kill me if I stop, so I keep playing louder and louder to match the fight, and then Josh jumps in and tries to separate them, but they continue to yell, then Nadine starts swinging her arms like a windmill coming toward Jen, who is still being held back by Josh and is punching the air like a boxer, and I match my staccato notes to her punches and then Jen breaks free from Josh and the momentum propels her into Nadine, who falls back on the ground, and she just lies there.

54

I RUN OUTSIDE and scream: "Oh my God! Nadine!"

Nadine is flat on the ground, repeating, "My ankle." Jen stands over her.

I look at Jen. "How dare you touch her? What were you thinking? You freak!"

And she looks me straight in the eyes and then runs inside.

I help Nadine back inside her house; she hops on one foot. My mom tells me later that Mrs. Ando took Nadine to Surrey Memorial Hospital. It feels so awesome to have done the right thing and helped.

It's Saturday. The phone rings. It's Nadine. "The frozen peas you put on the ankle really helped. Thanks," she says.

"Are you okay?"

"I'm okay, but I probably won't be able to dance for a few weeks."

"Oh no!" I say. And then I don't know what comes over me, but I continue, "Hey, prom is in a month; you'll be able to dance then. Wanna come? You never got a prom and all our friends will be there. It could be fun."

"Sure," she says. And I'm finally realizing that this will be a great, full-circle moment. We will go to prom together, then we will be in the same school next year, and everything will be fine. Like all we had to do was get through this year. I got everything I wanted. I won.

That night, I stand in the shower. I've just started showering instead of taking baths because that's what grown-ups do and that's what Nadine does. Actually, real grown-ups, like my mom and dad, take showers in the morning. I haven't started doing that yet.

Bottles of shampoo line the edge of the tub. I bought all of these using my allowance. I can't seem to find shampoo that will make my hair smooth and shiny like Nadine's or the girls in the commercials on TV. My hair is just the same kinda curly and frizzy mess as always, and I feel like I've been swindled.

I vow to myself that I will shower in the mornings. Starting tomorrow. Maybe that will help make my hair smoother, especially if I blow-dry it.

55

MOM IS DRIVING me and James to a piano competition. I don't really feel like going, but it's too late now. We've already crossed the bridge. The only good thing about piano competitions is that they are downtown. I love the drive downtown. I always bring a book with me because the trip is pretty long, like forty minutes or so. Though I never end up reading the book because it kind of makes me carsick, so I just look out the window instead. We always drive along the freeway, by the farms, and I like watching the cows lying around, taking a nap; they're pretty cool.

And then I see it, the best part: Vancouver's sunset. A baby pink sky folding over peach buildings, down into a powder blue ocean. Like one big pastel smudge in the sky.

We walk into the Queen Elizabeth Theatre. All the usual kids are there: the girl who always wears frilly party dresses (pink this year), the girl who always wears jeans

(Mom always shakes her head in disapproval), and the boy with dark hair who's a lot older, like sixteen, who always plays jazz. He's so dreamy.

I'm backstage, alone, except for a man in a suit and a light blue tie. I'm not quite sure why he is there. He's not holding a clipboard or anything. He's just smiling at me.

I hear my name being called and quickly walk across the stage to the baby grand. Adjust the bench so it is the right distance from the piano, just as Mrs. West told me. I sit. I breathe.

I start, and it's amazing how my fingers know where to go and how I don't really have to think about what to do, they just do it, and I have total trust in my hands and all I have to do is feel when the music should be getting louder and softer; my face goes close to the keys when it's soft and I jerk up and press my fingers down hard when it goes loud—

I play the final note so soft, you can barely hear it.

I smile, and then they clap. And then I bow and move away so the next act can come on.

James and I approach the piano. We sit down. I'm on the right, he's on the left. I motion by nodding my head, *One, two, three.* And then we play.

We sound fantastic. I don't think anyone has ever

seen two pairs of hands work together so well, and I actually like sitting beside my brother and he's doing great and I'm really proud of him because this is a pretty hard piece for him, and I think maybe we could be famous one day, like a brother-sister duet sensation, and travel the world and play piano and—

James stops. Suddenly.

And I keep playing, waiting for him to jump back in, but he doesn't know how to because we never practiced that; whenever we screwed up we just started from the beginning, but you can't do that at piano competitions and so I just keep playing, hoping he'll come back and join in, but then I play the final note, which really isn't the final note because James was meant to play it.

We stand up. I put my hand on the piano and James takes my other hand and we bow together. Just like how Mrs. West taught us and just like how Mom made us practice over and over again.

We go back to our seats in the audience. He sits on one side of Mom, I sit on the other. And I say nothing to him, I'm so pissed off. Two blond sisters are now onstage playing and they're okay but not as good as we could have been if my stupid brother hadn't screwed it up. James reaches over and taps me on the arm and whispers, "I'm sorry, Sara. I'm so sorry. I got scared and just stopped."

I win a gold for my solo.

We win a bronze for the duet.

That man in the suit gave us our medals.

In the car, on our way home, I just look at James. And a tear rolls from under his nerdy glasses, down his cheek. He knows it's his fault we didn't win gold in the duet. And I say to him, "I hate you. You ruined my life. I'm never playing with you again. I hate playing piano."

I don't feel like doing this anymore. Like ever again. Playing piano with my brother. I'm not a kid anymore; I have a social life now! I just want to go hang out with my friends and be with people my own age.

56

WE'RE HAVING a sleepover at Scarlett's house. Grade seven girls only. We eat pizza and make cookies and do sit-ups while they bake and watch a horror movie and then watch another movie with a little kissing in it on late-night TV and then Scarlett turns off the TV and does what I thought was just a rumor.

She pulls out an actual copy of the class list (how did she get that?) and goes through it in alphabetical order to gossip about everyone in class. Starting with *A*, of course.

"Jen Ando," Scarlett says.

And then people start saying things like:

"Oh my God, she thinks she is so smart!"

And "Yeah, like, get rid of the bowl haircut already!"

And "Yeah, what girl skateboards?!"

Scarlett looks at me and says, "Sara, what do you think? Are you friends with her?"

And I just look at everyone and say, "Don't know her too well. I'm just friends with her sister."

We go into Scarlett's older sister Sylvia's room. All her clothes are in giant piles on the floor. Scarlett digs around and puts some things in my backpack. "She won't notice. Take them home. Just give them back to me later."

The next Monday when Mom drops me off at school, I go straight to the girls' bathroom on the first floor. There, I meet Scarlett. I open my bag and put on her sister's clothes and get ready for class.

The bell rings.

I wear Sylvia's short skirt and Scarlett's black eyeliner. We walk into class together and everyone looks. And then I see Jen and she just rolls her eyes. What is her problem? Whatever, I don't need her, either.

After, I walk down the hall to the washroom in my borrowed platform heels. I stand in a stall for the rest of the day, and lean up against the wall. Nobody notices. I don't feel like learning anyway.

57

IT'S THE DAY before the science fair. I realize I do need to work on the project and get a good mark so I don't actually fail science at this point. I knock on the Andos' door. Jen answers and says, "What?"

"Hello? We should probably work on the science project since tomorrow is the fair," I say.

"Yeah, well, I have been working on it while you've been busy curling your eyelashes and dressing like a ho with Scarlett Davies," she says.

Me: "I am not dressing like a ho."

Her: "Yes you are, look at you; you're a ho."

"You're just jealous because you will never look like this," I say.

"No, I'm not, believe me."

"Well, we better work on the project or else we'll fail," I say.

"You might fail, but I won't."

"What do you mean?"

"You're out," she says. "It's my project now."

"What?"

"Yeah, you've barely helped. I'm just going to tell Monsieur Tanguay the situation."

Me: "I've worked on it!"

Her: "No, you haven't. Instead of studying man-made environmental damages, you're creating them with all that aerosol hairspray you're using these days."

"Whatever. And as if. I use the pump-spray kind. Anyway, I've been busy planning grade seven prom!"

"Isn't that ironic, since you're going to end up failing grade seven anyway!"

And I just look at her and say, "Whatever." And I turn around and start to walk home with Jen yelling after me, "HO, HO, HO, MERRY CHRISTMAS!" and I keep walking and it's raining and my hair is getting soaked, but I don't care, I am so mad, and Jen runs after me until we are both standing in the middle of the cul-de-sac.

She looks at me. And I just look at her. Her hair is soaked too. I can feel the mascara dripping down my cheeks.

Jen: "Why are you doing this?"

"Doing what?"

"Acting like this?"

"Because I don't like you," I say. "You're annoying and loud and you think you know it all. I never liked you when we were little, and I don't like you now. I just became friends with you to get back at Nadine. You're a revenge friend."

And then Jen's eyes start to get all watery and I'm not sure if it's tears running down her face or raindrops but strange sounds start coming out of her mouth and it's clear she's crying. She is crying so hard that all she can say is, "Well, at least I'm a good person." She runs inside. I just stare at the Ando house.

"What is wrong with you guys!" I yell. "You're a bunch of stuck-up witches in there!"

Nadine comes out with an umbrella, wearing rain boots.

"What are you doing?" she says. "Why are you yelling outside my house?"

"I'm expressing an opinion," I say. "It's a free country."

"Well, we don't want to hear it. You did enough. You made my sister cry," she says.

"I didn't make her cry. She made herself cry. I just came over to work on a school project. How dare you accuse me of anything, you hypocrite!"

"What is that supposed to mean?"

"Really? Hmm . . . let me think. Let's start with abandoning your best friend and betraying her and using her to buy clothes all while you knew you were leaving me. Let's start there."

"I didn't abandon you. I just went to a different school. You're the one who became friends with my younger sister to rub it in my face. Everyone can see it. It's sad. How dare you use her as a pawn in some game you think you're playing against me!"

"I'm not playing a game," I say. "Though your sister can be annoying as hell, she's a way better person than you. At least she is loyal. You think you're so great, walking around in your ballet bun and doing grade eight math. You're not that great. You're a selfish human being for what you did."

"Leave my sister and my family alone, you psycho. Get off our driveway, now," Nadine says. She keeps walking forward and pushes me off her driveway. Once I'm off, she walks back inside and closes the door, and my body is trembling in shock that my old best friend pushed me like that. I hate them. I wish I never knew them.

58

AT HOME, MOM is watching me eat. She just sits there, across the kitchen table, watching me chew. I hate her. I hate everyone in my life. I know what she's about to say.

"Why don't you practice piano?"

"Don't put your backpack on the floor."

"Put your dish in the sink."

"Sit up straight and wear socks and put lotion on your face."

I am trapped. I cannot talk with my mouth full. She knows this.

I finally swallow and say, "I need a new dress for graduation."

"Wear what you wore to Josh's bar mitzvah party," she says.

"Everyone saw that one, and everyone else will have new dresses."

"Who do you think you are, a millionaire?" she says.

Me: "It's the most important day of my life!"

Her: "It's not the most important day of your life."

"Yes, it is!"

"Maybe you should study more. How is science class going?"

Me: "Don't change the subject! I know what you're doing. Nice try!"

"My point is you should focus on school, not dresses. Use your brain!"

I copy her accent: "Okay, I will use my bLLLaine. Learn how to speak English."

Mom is quiet. She looks at me like she doesn't recognize me anymore. She says nothing. I run upstairs.

I pull clothes out of my drawers and shove them into my backpack.

I have no one, not even my mom, not even Nadine, not even Jen.

I switch off my lights and sit on my bed for an hour to fake that I'm sleeping. Once the noises in the house stop and everyone has gone to bed, I sling the backpack over my shoulder, open my door quietly, and tiptoe downstairs into the kitchen, grabbing the emergency flashlight from a drawer and the TV blanket from the couch. I slip out the side door and walk as silently as I can until I'm in the cul-de-sac looking up past the streetlights at the moon, then I run down the street.

The forest looks like the shadows of trees, or ghosts, not real trees. No, don't think about that now.

I point the flashlight down the path and stomp forward. I move the light from side to side like a strobe at a school dance, trying to scare everything around me, mainly the animals. I hear them (probably just rats and rabbits, right?) scurrying around in the bushes, trying to get the heck away from me. It's strange to think that just behind me, only meters away, people are snug in their beds, sound asleep, because in here, in Green Timbers Forest, everything is awake.

It's darker inside the forest and I can't see much, even with the flashlight. I crouch to the ground and feel around for a stick, but my backpack pushes up and I lose balance and fall over. But it's okay, because I find a stick in the process that I use to get up and I poke around like a blind person as I walk down what I think is a path, but it's probably just straight-up bush because it feels like needles scraping the sides of my jeans and almost poking me in the eyes.

I look up at the roof of dark trees above me, hoping for some moonlight to shine through, but something hits my head and I fall down.

Ouch. That hurt a lot.

I see two flashes of light in the distance, like someone

is signaling to me. I crawl through the shrub toward the flashes, which look more like spotlights reflecting off a massive mirror into my eyes. Maybe it's aliens, like on that show.

An opening, a clearing in the forest:

The bright moon above shines on a black metallic lake and I stop because my head hurts. I touch my forehead and it's a bit wet. I can tell it's blood. I'm bleeding quite a lot.

I continue, crawling up to the edge of the water, and flip over and look up to the sky. The back of my head is up against some rocks, but I don't care, I just want to lie here. I stare up and it looks like someone poked a million little holes in a black blanket and the brightest light is pouring through them.

It reminds me of camping in the backyard and looking up at the sky with Nadine and Jen. I start to cry.

Why did I say those awful things? Why did I act that way? Why did I try to be smarter, more grown-up? Why did I become friends with Jen just because Nadine was no longer there? I used Jen. I'm so mean. She's actually a really good person, and to be honest, we get along better than me and Nadine. I was terrible to them all. To Jen, Nadine, my brother, my mom especially. One day, they will die and I'll wish I was nicer.

My cries echo through the clearing. I remember hearing

about this place. Daniel mentioned it to James. Then I remember the abandoned search for him in the forest. And how I used him and the search to try to get Nadine back. What kind of horrible person does that? What kind of person uses a missing boy as a ploy to get a friend back? I think about that poor kid. He's probably out there, sitting in the dark somewhere, in a room, or in the ground, not knowing where he is or what happened to him. I think, why doesn't someone just kidnap me? I'm the one who doesn't deserve to be here. I'm the one who doesn't deserve to live.

"Come get me! I'm here! Take me!" I yell.

I hear a rustling close by and flinch. Oh no, I take it back, I take back my wish. I sit up and turn around and see the silhouette of a boy.

Wait.

"Daniel?"

Ahead, I see him running toward the forest.

"Daniel! Come back!"

I start running after him, into the forest, but he zig-zags deeper into it, and I lose him. Then I see something moving behind a bush and I jump on him and we fall on the ground and lie there for a bit, my arms around him, as I catch my breath.

I found him, I found Daniel Monroe, I'm holding him down so he doesn't leave ever again. I will bring him home to his mom and she will . . .

"Sara?"

It's not Daniel.

"James, what are you doing here?"

"I followed you," James says. "I figured you left to look for him here, finally. I care about him too. He was my friend too."

"I'm sorry, James."

"I made him feel bad that day at the baseball game when we messed up that play."

"James, it's not your fault."

"He was my friend, Sara. He was going to be my best friend. I know it."

I just hold James a bit and rock back and forth and he sobs. After a few seconds he says, "Do you know where we are?"

"I'm not sure. I can't really see and I lost my flash-light."

"I'm so scared," he says.

"It'll be okay," I say.

"I think your head is bleeding, Sara."

"It's fine. We'll be fine."

I say this for my little brother's sake, even though I'm not sure if we will be fine. I feel around on my hands and knees in the darkness and find a big tree trunk to put our backs up against. I still have my backpack, miraculously, and pull the TV blanket over us. "Let's just stay here until the sun comes up a bit so we can see well enough to get home," I say.

"Sara, do you think someone really took him? Like a bad guy?"

"I don't know. Let's not worry about that right now. It'll only freak us out," I say. "I love you, James."

I sit there under a fir tree holding my little brother, unsure of what just happened but hoping that the sun will rise soon.

Lights in my eyes. But it's not the stars or the sun, it's the same light from the orthodontist and for a moment, I think it's him, Dr. Chiang, but it's not. It's Mr. Ando. "I found them!" he shouts, then another light flashes back and forth and Dad appears. Dad scoops me up and Mr. Ando gets James. As Dad carries me out of the forest, I whisper in his ear, "I couldn't keep us all together."

Dad stops and cradles me in his arms. He says softly, "It's okay, Sara. I love you."

I wake up in my parents' bed, in between Mom and Dad. James is here too. We haven't all been in bed together since James and I were really little, like babies.

James is sleeping. I can tell Mom is still awake because she isn't snoring (she usually does).

I say, "I'll never say those things or run away again. I'm sorry."

"I know," Mom says. "You're a good girl."

"I don't want you guys to die! Please don't die and leave me!" I'm crying, but I'm trying to stop myself by holding my breath. Mom holds me and says, "Just let it out, Sara. Breathe and cry. It's good to let it out. To be heard. It's healthy."

Once she says this, I magically stop for a bit. I look up at her and notice she's not wearing lipstick. It's the first time I've seen her like this. She looks even more beautiful. I stare at the tiny diamond stud in her ear and fall asleep under her star.

59

I COME DOWN the stairs to the kitchen and see that Nadine is sitting at our kitchen table eating ddukbokki. Rice cakes in the shape of solid tubes mixed in with green onions and red spicy sauce that kind of looks like lava. Mom's ddukbokki is the best and everyone who eats it feels better.

Nadine looks taller than usual sitting at the table. Like it's lower than it should be. Then I realize she hasn't been at my house since last summer. She stands up suddenly when she sees me.

"Are you okay?"

I'm surprised she cares. And that she is even here.

"I heard you were almost kidnapped."

"Not really, I was just in the forest, trying to get kidnapped," I say.

She looks a little disappointed. I sit down in front of her. Mom gently slides a plate of ddukbokki in front of me. I prick one with my fork and eat the chewy noodle and feel instantly better.

Nadine puts a small box in front of me. It's wrapped in pink tissue paper with gold ribbon tied around it.

"I never gave this to you. . . . It's your birthday present," she says. "I'm sorry I didn't get it to you sooner. But your birthday was when Daniel went missing and I forgot about it after because I wasn't thinking straight. Also, I thought you kind of hated me after I told you about skipping and I was afraid to mention it and the more time passed, the more awkward it got. . . ."

I pull the wrapping off slowly, kind of scared of what could be inside.

It's one half of a broken heart of a silver best friend necklace. Nadine pulls down the collar of her T-shirt. "See?" she says. "I'm wearing the other half."

I look down at the broken heart and think how well it describes our best friendship, and maybe all girl best friendships.

"Thanks, it's really nice of you," I say. "I'm really sorry about the other day. I shouldn't have said what I said. You were right, I was being a psycho."

"It's okay. I'm sorry too," she says. "That was really messed up of me, pushing you off our driveway like that."

"It's all good," I say. "I sort of deserved it."

And we sit there for a while, eating Mom's ddukbokki and being nice to each other. But the truth is, it doesn't feel that comfortable. She's changed. I have. And that's okay.

Later that night, I place the pendant in a bowl with my other jewelry. It doesn't feel right to wear it. She's not my forever best friend. My best friend is someone else.

60

IT'S THE SCIENCE FAIR. I show up at our booth with a small bandage on my forehead from falling. Jen is there. I see that she put both our names on the project. I guess she heard about what happened and feels sorry for me. When the judges come around, including Ms. Lee, we present our project. Jen does most of the talking. We win second place and get an A+.

After, I thank Jen for doing most of the work and tell her I can pack up the table myself and she can go home. She doesn't say too much but seems relieved that I offered. "It's the least I can do," I say.

Later that day, Nadine calls. She can't come to prom. I actually forgot I invited her. "My ankle still hurts," she says. "Plus, it doesn't feel like my prom. It might be a little weird."

I tell her that I understand, because I kind of do. Somehow it doesn't bother me at all that she won't be there.

61

IN THE PENCIL sharpener line. Josh is ahead of me. He turns around and blurts out, "Maybe we should go to prom together. Just as friends, you know."

"Okay," I say.

It's grade seven prom. It's at the Pacific Inn hotel, same place as Josh's bar mitzvah party. Scarlett wanted me to come over to her house and get ready with her. But I'm kind of sick of her. We just spent all day decorating the ballroom, and to be quite frank, she's boring.

Mom and Dad drive me to Josh's.

I'm wearing a magical white chiffon dress with pink butterflies all over it. Mom made it for me. It's super flowy and when I twirl, it whirls with me. I'm wearing makeup, too. Mom let me. Well, just lip gloss and mascara. A daisy is tucked behind my ear.

Josh opens the door. He smiles. Behind him his mother says, "You look beautiful, dear."

Our parents take pictures of us in their garden. Telling us to pose like this and that. Our parents drink wine and talk and Josh and I just kind of stand around.

At the prom:

Everyone just dances together, and sometimes I dance with Josh, and sometimes I dance with other boys in class, and sometimes I dance with girls, and I even dance with Ms. Lee, because it's our last dance ever of elementary school and it suddenly hits me that this may be the last time I ever see these people and I want to make sure to look at everyone and try to memorize one thing about them so I can remember something about them forever. But someone is missing. Someone should be here.

Later that night, coming home from prom, I see Jen in silhouette through her bedroom window, dancing by herself slowly. I think she wanted to be there too.

62

SO IT'S THE last day of school. And I got sent to the vice principal's office again. Actually, I kinda turned myself in. Thing is, I kinda punched Ricky in the face.

What happened: He snapped my bra so hard and I was so mad that I turned around too quickly and my arms kinda flailed into his face. His nose bled a bit. But he didn't care. He was embarrassed, if anything. He had tissues up his nose as plugs the rest of the day. I felt bad. No one else saw this happen.

So I am explaining all this to Ms. Lee and she sits on her desk and she smiles, puts up her hand, and says, "This is off the record but . . . high five." She gives me one. "Good for you. He totally deserved it, if you ask me."

Later, at home:

I read my yearbook, which is really just a photocopied booklet with everyone's pictures in it and some blank pages at the end for people to write messages on.

By reading them, I find out who left the perfume, the rose, the card, and the chocolates.

He wrote a message in my yearbook, next to his picture. It reads:

It was me. I asked your brother what you liked. I hope you liked the presents. Have a great summer. Luv, Ricky.

Sometimes, the truth surprises you so hard, you look up and the world looks really different. Like all the colors are off or something. I sit there, at the piano, with the yearbook open where music should be, staring at the message. Ricky? Really?

This means that for sure it wasn't Nadine or some creep.

I don't contact Ricky to say thank you or anything.

63

IT'S THE END of June and everyone smells like sunblock. Josh and I go to the pool together and tread water in the deep end. Kids are splashing all around us and I can barely keep my eyes open.

"Jen says hi," Josh says.

"Oh yeah?"

"We boarded together in Bear Creek Park the other day," he says.

Me: "Yah, I haven't really talked to her that much for a while. I think she hates me."

Josh: "I'm not so sure about that."

All the kids are still splashing water in our faces, so I close my eyes for a bit because they sting. I drop under the water and swim to the ladder and get out of the pool. My wet feet make a *splat splat splat* sound as I walk across the deck. I climb up to the highest diving board.

At the top:

I look all around and love the feeling of being so high. I look down, straight into Josh's eyes. We stare at each other for a while.

And then I jump.

64

"SARA IS AT the door," Mrs. Ando calls up.

She slips upstairs and I don't move from the front entrance. I can't. Maybe because the thought of Jen is something that has become foreign to me these past few weeks, or maybe I still feel bad for saying those mean things, or maybe because she doesn't know that I, too, cried that day after our fight in the middle of the cul-de-sac, it's just that she ran into her house first before she could see. But I'm here and I must go in.

Behind are the sounds of cul-de-sac, loud and clear: boys playing street hockey, the roar of passing cars, the hiss of timed sprinklers setting off. I close the door, muffling the street noises.

I stand still in the hallway because it's not like before when I would just walk right in and join her in whatever she was doing (once I even came into the bathroom while she was on the toilet). Things are different now. I ring the doorbell.

Jen is in the kitchen, standing at the counter. Her breaths are short, nervous.

"Come in," she says, without making eye contact. She is spreading peanut butter onto a piece of bread. I walk over.

"Hi," I say.

She says, "Want a sandwich?"

"Sure."

Her: "White bread or brown?"

Me: "I'm not prejudiced." She smiles slightly at this, still not looking at me. I could never spread the peanut butter without crumbling the bread under the knife. I think I press too hard. Jen spreads some perfectly for me. Must be in the Andos' DNA. She uses a small spoon to scoop up blackberry jam and put it on top.

"So how are you? What's new?" I ask, forcing a casual tone. We both know what I'm really asking.

"Not much," she says. "Oh, Nadine plucked her eyebrows on Sunday again. Her left eyebrow, like, disappeared. She and Mom made a frantic late-night run to the drugstore to buy this black eyebrow pencil. So now she has a thin, drawn-in left eyebrow."

Laughing, I say, "Been there, done that." There is a brief silence after this. I search for something new to say, but she beats me to it.

Jen: "I heard Ricky is the one who left you the gifts

and that he liked you. Doesn't make up for the fact that he basically sexually harassed you. Boys are so messed up."

"Yeah," I say.

"How's Josh?"

"Good," I say. "We're going to the fair tomorrow." Pause. "You want to come?"

"No," she says. "I'm busy, you know, our whole family is."

I say, "I saw the sign on the lawn."

Jen: "Yeah, it's all happening so fast. There's a lot of new stuff I haven't told you about."

"But moving . . ." I trail off.

"Mom's pregnant."

"What?"

"Yeah," Jen says, pacing around. "They told us in the lamest way, too. Nadine and I were setting the table for dinner one night, then Dad was like, 'Pretty soon you girls will have to set an extra place.' It was really obvious and cheesy." Jen shakes her head.

We sit down together at the table and share a crunchy peanut butter and jelly feast.

"But moving?" I ask again.

"They say we need a bigger house, with the new baby and all. They already found a buyer."

"Yeah, I saw the 'Sold' sign."

"They said something about the market being really

good, or maybe it's really bad, I'm not sure. Anyway, we're moving to Sunshine Hills. We're going to a new school, too. We move at the end of the summer."

"That's pretty soon," I say. My eyes start to sting and fill with water. Jen sees this and hugs me.

This is where I lose it. I start crying so hard that I can't breathe, and when I realize that I can't breathe, it makes it worse. I tell her that I'm sorry: sorry for calling her a revenge friend, sorry for pushing her aside when we were little to play with Nadine, sorry for all the things I've ever done to hurt her or to make her feel less than me.

"It's okay," Jen whispers. "Nothing is going to change."

But we both know this is a lie, because things always change. Still, it sounds better and feels better to say this, to pretend to believe it. I let her hug me, smelling peanut butter on her breath. I think, *We'll just stay like this for a while, me crying and Jen hugging, until we feel like letting go. . . .*

It's August and the Ando family has officially moved out of the cul-de-sac.

The letter Jen Ando sent me, the one with no stamp on it, sits on the piano. The neighborhood sprinklers are shooting away like little water guns outside.

I remember how, while driving me to school or when peeling apples for us, Mom would say, "Enjoy your life now. This is your golden time."

Now I kinda get what she was saying. There is no rush to grow up and skip grades and get boyfriends and shave legs, because being a kid is the best. I had the best childhood, and I have the Ando family to thank for that.

I can hear an ice cream truck in the distance, getting louder and louder. The sun is starting to set and I can see the moon starting to rise.

When I think about everything that's happened this year, and everyone I said good-bye to, I understand that it wasn't really about losing Cookie or Daniel or Nadine or Jen or the entire Ando family, it was about being okay with things changing and feeling true sadness for the first time.

I stare at the letter and sort of wonder if it'll be the last letter I receive from her. I doubt it. Though we don't talk every day anymore, Jen and I do keep in touch. And although they have moved out of the cul-de-sac, the Ando family will never move out of my life, right? These people who were so important to me will always have a place in my heart, won't they? I hope so. Even if I don't see them as much, or hardly at all, in the future. Regardless, I'll always be okay.

Even today, in a crowd, like in the mall or downtown on Robson Street, walking down to English Bay to see the fireworks, I'll see a blond boy ahead of me and I will still find myself running up behind him to casually pass him, and turn to look, hoping it's Daniel.

And sometimes, like when I'm practicing piano and there's a knock at the door, there is this little part of me that hopes that it'll be the Ando sisters, wanting to play, saying there's a rainbow in the sky.

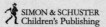

Don't miss any of these amazing novels from the winner of the National Book Award and the Newbery Medal,

CYNTHIA KADOHATA:

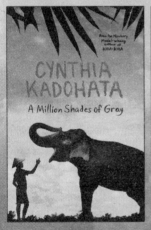